charity

by Mark Richard

The Ice at the Bottom of the World
Fishboy
Charity

Anchor Books ⚓ Doubleday

New York   London   Toronto   Sydney   Auckland

charity

stories

mark richard

AN ANCHOR BOOK
PUBLISHED BY DOUBLEDAY
a division of Random House, Inc.
1540 Broadway, New York, New York 10036

ANCHOR BOOKS, DOUBLEDAY, and the portrayal
of an anchor are trademarks of Doubleday, a division of
Random House, Inc.

Charity was first published in the United States by Nan A. Talese/
Doubleday in 1998.

BOOK DESIGN BY T. KARYDES

The stories in this collection have appeared, in slightly different
form, in the following publications as follows: "Gentleman's
Agreement," "Where Blue Is Blue," and "Fun at the Beach" in
Esquire; "Plymouth Rock" in *Grand Street*; "The Birds for Christmas"
in *The New Yorker*; "Charity" and "Never in This World" in *Harper's*;
"Charming 1 br, Fr. dr. wndws, quiet, safe. Fee." in *The Literary
Insomniac: Stories and Essays for Sleepless Nights*; "Tunga Tuggo, Lingua
Dingua" in *The Paris Review*; and "Memorial Day" in *The Oxford
American*.

The Library of Congress has cataloged the hardcover edition of this
book as follows:

Richard, Mark, 1955–
    Charity: stories / Mark Richard. — 1st ed.   p.   cm.
    Contents: Gentlemen's agreement — Where blue is blue —
Plymouth Rock — The birds of Christmas — Fun at the beach —
Charity — Charming 1 BR, FR, DR, WNDWS, quiet, safe, fee —
Never in this world — Tunga tuggo, lingua dingua — Memorial
Day.
    1. United States—Social life and customs—20th century—
Fiction. I. Title.   PS3568.I313C48   1998
813'.54—DC21   98-10317   CIP

FIC RIC

ISBN 0-385-42570-8

First Anchor Books Edition: September 1999

1 2 3 4 5 6 7 8 9 10

JENNIFER, ROMAN, RAY

contents

charity

gentleman's agreement

The child had been warned. His father said he would nail that rock-throwing hand to the shed wall, saying it would be hard to break windshields and people's windows with a hand nailed to the shed wall. Wouldn't it? said his father, home for a few hours from the forest he could not extinguish. Goddamn it, didn't the child know what windshields costed? His father held the child up by his ear to better see the spiderweb burst of windshield glass. All the clawing child could better see were the rivets holding his father's smoke-smelling pants together.

Even the child could not understand how the windshield had happened, the child that morning playing splay-legged in the dusty rough driveway, dripping seed-size gravel from a tiny hour-glass of fist, flipping a fake stone kernel to a crow come flying down to watch, and the crow not fooled, flapping back away, taking flight when the child rained sand, the child splashing around in the dirt like a seaside idiot, rock droplets up in the air, into the smoky sky that was white like broken melon rind and smelled like the old man's beard and breath.

A playmate had sprung up from the ground near the gully where the good rocks grew, and they began gauging themselves against themselves again, lessons of arc and tra-jectory, the specific nature of things spinning farther today than yesterday in that white-rind sky, until one rock left the child's fingers while his mind was on something else, this rock on a course that even the playmate ceased fire to regard.

Time slowed for them, the rock arcing toward the friendly family car parked pleasantly in the pecan tree shade. Time slowed and slowed. If time had not slowed, the rock would have sailed over the car, over the pecan tree, over the rented house, and over the town and the burning forests beyond. But the world was enormous that morning, its gravity immense. To arc and trajectory add the lessons of apogee and descent, the rock descending into a broken-glass poke in the eye for the friendly family car, the play-mate suddenly skipping away dropping stones, skipping away to slither, laughing, along the gully home.

All afternoon the rind sky lowered and smelled of burning woods.

Goddamn it! Didn't the child know what windshields costed? His father in his dirty, roughed-up denim, of all days to come home, mud and ash, machete on the hip and the snake pistol, timber boots laced with wire that wouldn't burn, the blackened shanks of ankles, the boot soles cracked by heat and desperate shoveling, his father footprinting crazy mazes of topography across the clean wooden floors.

Goddamn it, what was in that head his father shook in his hands like a snow globe? Nothing, said the child, and in his heart the words of the covenant: Never, ever throw another rock ever, again. Ever.

In those days the fire went south and the old man was gone again, sleeping in woods and fields the flames had not yet found. The child posted himself at the top of the rough driveway and waited for his father's truck, pious with an unbroken covenant in his heart, no stone had touched his fingers, no rock had he held. He knew his mother was watching him wait for his father from the front window of the rented house. He had heard her wonder if her husband would ever come home again.

On a Saturday afternoon when it did not seem like his father was ever coming home, the child stood at the top of the rough driveway, watching a mule pull a wagon full of black men past the rented house into town. A black man sitting on the tailgate of the wagon extended a middle finger toward the child and the child waved back. The wind was keeping the smoke out of town that day and the child decided to go lie in the gully and pretend he was dead in a battlefield trench.

The child walked down the washed-out driveway, shirtless, Indian-brown, and barefoot, scuffing along until a baby-headed tomahawk stone revealed itself in the dust. The child stopped and poked at the stone with his toe. The child poked at the stone and worried the stone with his toe until the stone was free in the driveway dirt. The child searched the covenant in his heart and discovered nothing about just *kicking* a stone, so the child kicked the baby-headed tomahawk stone to the end of the driveway where the grass was tall and dense, uncut by his absent father. There was nothing in the covenant, nothing in the agreement the child had in his heart with his father about just *picking up a stone over grass*, that's all it was, so the child just picked up the stone to carry it over the grass to the gully where he could look at it while pretending to be dead in a battlefield trench.

But just picking up the stone from its place in the common earth seemed to signify the stone somehow, and it would probably be best to put it in a special place. Not to throw, never to throw, because that would break the agreement in the heart with the father, but just to put the stone away somewhere to consider it later, maybe even as a test to never, ever throw another rock ever again. So the child carried the stone to the tin-roofed shed. There was nothing in the covenant about just *carrying a stone into a shed as an example of the child's goodness.* There was a box in the shed where the child could hide the stone. To study later. And when he grew up and was older than the old man, he could even shake the thing up to the old man's face and say, *See? Here* is a rock I *didn't* throw!

In the tin-roofed shed was the lawn mower his father used to cut the ragged yard. There were the broken fire tools the father brought home to fix. On a nail hung a drip of steel helmet melted by a mad-dog fire that had chased the father hatless across three firebreaks, had chased him into a steaming river, had run him through an orange-and-red ravine where his father dove into the ragged mouth of a cave, and his father crawled as deep as he could crawl into that worst-smelling place until he crawled on top of a bear trying to crawl as deep as it could crawl away from the mad-dog fire that was barking at the mouth of the cave to come in. His father and the bear crawled to the fartherest corner of the cave and curled up together, the bear hugging his father and calling out and crying the worst you've ever heard, said his father, because she had left her cub out in the orange-and-red ravine where the mad-dog fire was barking and where the world was coming to an end.

And in the tin-roofed shed the child saw where the Goat should have been parked—the Goat, the big, yellow fire bike, the marble-size knobs on the tire treads, the homemade steel-mesh cages the old man had welded around the chain and spokes against brush and branches, his father riding the Goat's back in wild reconnaissance of the fire's forward lines, and on Sundays when the world was not on fire the old man and his disciples drank beer in the backyard and rode the Goat down the washed-out driveway fast enough to leap the gully, doing drunken doughnuts and wheelies in the cornfield until somebody's wife went home mad or until somebody broke his arm and thought it was funny.

Considering the spot where the Goat should have

been parked warmed the baby-headed tomahawk stone in the child's hand until there was no comfortable way to hold it.

It was much easier to hold the stone behind the tin-roofed shed where there was nothing of his father's to see, nothing to see at all except oceans of corn you would need a ship to cross. Behind the tin-roofed shed was the pile of rocks from the time the landlord tore down the old well house, and the child was never to go near where the old well house had been, he and his father had a handshake agreement about that, he was never to go near the place in the ground that was covered with thick planks; there were snakes down there and the hole was bottomless and even the child knew how bottomless it was by all the sticks and tree limbs he had shoved down between the planks trying to stir the snakes up to the surface.

The child had to decide how to hide his stone to distinguish it from all these other common well-house rocks piled behind the tin-roofed shed. The rotten lean of the place put the edge of the tin roof within the child's reach if he stood on the pile of common rocks, so he did, he climbed the rock pile and reaching up he could almost hide his stone on the roof if he could just toss it up there, not throw it, that was not what he was going to do, but to just toss the stone up on the roof to distinguish it from the other common rock-pile rocks, putting the stone in a special place, keeping it for later.

It was a cheap gunshot noise the child made when he tossed the stone up on the tin-roofed shed, not artillery or anything apocalyptic yet, just a nice, good, gunfight-starting shot, and immediately the common rocks in the rock pile the child was standing on were jealous, he could feel them jealous under his feet. They wanted to be not rocks but rockets, rockets and artillery, and the child said, Okay, just a couple, tossing a couple of rocks is not like throwing a couple of rocks where windshields and people's windows break. He was just being nice to the common well-house rocks.

So the child began to heave the rocks from the rock pile he was standing on up onto the tin roof of the shed. It was a gunfight and a battle and a war, the way they bounced and blew up on the roof, bouncing and clattering around, he worked his way through the pistols and the rifles, bending and tossing, bending and tossing, not waiting until the din had dimmed, but keeping rocks in the air, bouncing and banging. Rockets! the child tossed, Hangernades! until the large keystone of the well house was uncovered and the child said, Adam bomb! and the child had to heave the heavy rock with both hands with all of that day's strength, and in his strength his foot slipped on the loose rocks and the child slipped off the rock pile. The doomsday rock failed to clear the edge of the roof. Down it came square on top of the fallen child's crew-cut head.

the best white doctor in town was the abortionist up the wooden steps across from the courthouse. It was sticky hot, and the doctor slept stuck to the dirty exam-table paper. Flawless liftoffs from Florida tarmac, warm pulpy orange juice, the cool white spread of oscillating fan across the naked backs of Nurse Bedpan's legs, these the morphine dreams of an ex–flight surgeon, grounded, a rough shuddering landing from his sleep when the friendly green family car jumps the sidewalk curb just outside and crushes in the corner of the doctor's wooden building, so difficult to see to drive when the windshield is shattered in bright and opaque pieces, the mother's head out the window to see to steer, one hand on the steering wheel and the other keeping constant pressure on the pretty pink ruined towel turban-wrapped around the child's head, driving a shift, too, more balls than all of us, the old man would say about her,

her driving, her springing young black men from their places on the sidewalk where they have come by mule wagon and on foot to loiter and to spit, black bucks jumping back from the kneecap-crushing fender-leveled friendly green family car, the front end rattling the doctor from where he had bid sweet Morpheus take him to his beloved Nurse Bedpan, the fender rattling the old building and the old building's rainspout and gutters where the nightwings hid, the bats behind there, bats hanging by the hundreds and thousands over Main Street all day long if you really looked for them, gone at night flitting for the ton or two of mosquitoes the ballpark ditches and third-base mud hole yielded in the evenings, but back during the day and you could see them if you really looked for them, a tiny wing here and there folded over a bent rain gutter, that long line of black tar caulking the roof beams, not really caulking at all, just the tops of thousands of tiny heads hanging upside down along the eaves and roofline, at least one shaken awake by the crash that woke the doctor, awake now and cotton-mouthed, a fleeting face in the ceiling corner of his favorite flyboy, the one endowed with extraterrestrial hand-eye and an irritating venereal drip.

Creatures were stirred, creatures were stirring, and en route to the doctor's, through a gap in the wrapping of the turban towel, the child had studied the tiny pebbles stuck in the green rubber floor mat of the family car, excruciating corduroy design was all he could see, was all that was his focus, those tiny pebbles stuck in the long green rubber lines. He had felt the collision of friendly car and drain spout, had felt himself being pulled across the seat, and then he could see his blood-mottled dusty feet down through the slit in his towel wrap, he saw his feet take a step up a curb. There was a splattering of tobacco chew beside his mother's foot, the pressure of her hand tightened on the towel over the spot where his head had broken open. He felt her pressure on the towel on his head and her other hand leading him to a wooden step leading to another wooden step leading up, and then suddenly he heard her scream, and he heard men laughing, and he felt the towel fall away because she was not holding it any longer and he felt the towel fall like a mantle onto his shoulders, and the light was white to his turbaned eyes as he squinted, and just after he felt the wet towel fall to his shoulders something else fell, and it fell flapping against his neck where the blood ticked dripping from his broken-open head and the thing that fell against his neck felt like tickling fingers, and still blinded he shrugged it off and it fell at his feet, and it flapped around and shrieked at his toes and his eyes focused on the thing and he heard his mother screaming and he heard men laughing and someone caught him and lifted him up the wooden stairs before he went into a different kind of sleep that day.

the child was sitting in cold bathwater worrying about bats falling out of his head again when they finally brought his father home. The large sanitary napkin the doctor had taped to the top of the child's head was now dirty and ragged, the doctor saying not to wash his hair for two weeks until the stitches came out, and now it had been two weeks and the stitches itched to come out, or at least something felt like it was scratching its little black claws in the child's scalp to come out. The child did not trust the stitches to hold against the bats and was hoping they would not break while his mother was around because he was sure it would frighten her to see things falling out of his head again, and what if they didn't just fall out but flew around the house getting into the curtains? The doctor had been eager to get back to his dreaming and even the child knew he had done a hurry-up job on his head, the mother saying later that the doctor's sewing was better suited for patching a Mexican blanket, the doctor even forgetting to be paid until the mother insisted on a bill and the doctor wrote some numbers on a piece of yellow paper and then locked the door behind them so he could needle himself back to that place with the white patio, him in his white uniform, the nurse with the white breasts he loved so much, that white place, the white sand, those white waves.

When they brought his father into the hallway, the child did not recognize him at first. His father was missing his hair on his head and his eyebrows were gone and his beard had melted into little black knots on his skin. He had been the only one left, they said. They told the mother in the hall that it was as if the father had refused to burn when everyone else they found had turned into short, black, shriveled roasts of people. The child's father was wearing just a ladies' raincoat that was clear plastic and wouldn't stick to the burns you could see that were red and raw and black on the father's back and arms. The father's hands were packed in grease and wrapped in gauze and the child wondered if those hands would even be able to hold a hammer to nail a rock-throwing hand to the shed wall. The child stood over his parents' bed for a long time, watching his father sleep in the room that smelled like a curing barn.

13

On Sunday on their way to the shed the father gathered his tools and showed the child his reckoning, his little column of figures, his carryovers, his paperwork. The white papers were windows and windshield. The yellow paper was the doctor. The little green stub was what they paid the father for keeping the fire from coming into town. By the father's figuring, he didn't think he could afford to keep the child, could not keep him in glass at least. It had been two weeks, but there were to be no more trips to Doctor Duck, the Quack, he called him. The rock-throwing hand had finally costed the father more than he had earned.

Sorry, said the father.

At the shed the father opened his toolbox and told the child it would be all right to holler if it hurt, that the child's hollering probably wouldn't bother anybody. It was Sunday and the mother had gone to church. The father rattled the tools around in his toolbox, poking around with his clawed fingers. The child had closed his eyes and when he smelled his father standing beside him, he lifted up his rock-throwing hand.

Here we go, said the father, and with his shears and his pliers the father set to work on the child's head, snipping and tugging at the black silky thread that had bound together the torn flesh of his only son.

where
blue is blue

This last time the carnival came to our town we had the contortionist in the inlet. Not exactly all of the contortionist. Somehow she had been sucked into the dredge boom that sweeps back and forth chewing sand underwater to keep the inlet open. Pieces of our contortionist were funneled along the spillway pipeline and were pumped in spume to nourish a washaway beach. What all morning a lifeguard at Fifth Street had thought was a big red jellyfish turned out to be something better identified by a doctor from Dayton, Ohio, out beachcombing with his son. The largest piece anyone had found so far by the time Cecil of our police got down there was a leg with a knot of intestine hung to it. A colored man was holding it against the current next to the dredge with a long-handled crab net. There were so many crabs all over that leg you could hardly make out the tattoos. Us we all who saw it lost our taste for crabmeat the rest of that summer.

There was no certain idea at the time how the contortionist came to be in the inlet, whether she had jumped the inlet bridge or had been pushed or if there was something else to it altogether. We all knew it was her, though, by what remained of the leg tattoos the crabs hadn't eaten off. You would be surprised how deep tattoos get into the skin. Cecil had his notebook, looking; the rest of us hired ourselves out for the job no one else wanted, breaking down the dredge teeth to search for more evidence. You could tell by the way Cecil watched us, sketching in his notebook, that he thought there was something else to this thing altogether.

Cecil, our one friend in the police, the deck-shoe detective with his sketch pad and paint book. All our oceanfront crime, all our oceanfront criminals. Coked-up busboys with steak knives, strangulation games by tourists taken a tightness too far. Seamy little deeds on vacation with evidence slipping away with every turn of the tide. The unidentified dead, homicides away from home, sometimes solvable by Cecil with just a postcard sketch and a drink with the linen maid.

Yes, Cecil, we had all seen the contortionist. *Seen* is an easy word for men like us. In her stuffy tent we saw more of her at once in one angle than we could ever see even of ourselves or the people we get to sleep with us. Like in a painting where everything is shown at once, everything unfolded and flat and impossible. We all stepped close to see more, and her stare kept us back, something in her eyes steady beyond the flicker of lamplight across her face. The more she showed us the more we saw there was no approach to her, nothing to touch that wasn't something else. Her tattooed legs became draping snakes around her neck, her hands kicking feet, her tongue a finger from her mouth pulling through narrows of flesh. Her eyes always on yours until you had to turn away and feel them still burn where they bore into your neck, her eyes we paid to conjure until we couldn't bear it and the tent canvas would bellows in and out about us, men coughing and lighting cigarettes coming out, shaking trouser legs, taking quick steps away from where we had been in this thing together.

Yes, everyone had seen her the last night when she disappeared, even Cecil, Cecil in the back of the tent, once when I had to look away from what the girl was showing. There was Cecil standing next to the carny bouncer where the canvas was knotted against the night, Cecil with his notebook open and sketching. We had also seen the contortionist when we didn't know it was her, us skulking around the carnival for the odd job, taking her for a man in long-sleeve khaki and long khaki pants, a man's hat pulled low over her face, not a scratch of tattoo to show. We saw her when we hustled her boyfriend to buy the scraps from around the docks we worked, things to feed the reptiles he wrestled, big fish guts, shark livers, yellow, and bags of fins. We would hang around to watch the boy-friend feed the big lizards, sissing them out of the low cages and scuffed wooden boxes, kicking open latches with his cowboy boots, the big lizards pressing through the burnt-up grass of the old town lot. They would press around the boyfriend as he fed them from the bags of guts we had brought, the girl in a magic trance watching, cooing them closer to angle their cold eyes to her, fish guts hung in their throats until they scrambled and gaped for more, us jump-ing the fence to get out of their way.

We had stood there next to the girl in khaki never knowing it was her until the day we showed up with a bottle of scotch and a bag of glue fumes we wanted to share with the boyfriend, and a long sleeve of khaki shot its cuffs into the circle where we were and a spider-sketched hand at the end of a serpent-stained wrist knocked what we offered away. Please don't, she said, and we saw it was her taking the boyfriend away for him to feed something else for her to watch. A carny came by and wrapped the paper sack around his face and lung-sucked the boyfriend's share of fumes. The carny told us that when the boyfriend gets high he tries to erase the girl's tattoos with forks and broken glass. We passed the bag and watched the girl make her rounds, laying out feed and filling water; the toothless lions gummed and licked her, the rainbow animal snatched her against its cage to make another kiss.

These were the ways we had seen the contortionist until this day when we put what we could of her into plastic bags with numbers, packages of her we laid in an ice chest on the deck of the barge. Cecil shuffled through them, looking. There were some parts we didn't find, some parts no one wanted to find. We all thought we had seen more of the contortionist at her last show than we would ever see but the bags in the ice chest proved us wrong, bags full of us working in dark, waist-deep water inside the muddy conveyor boom, flashlights stuck in our teeth with sick suspense.

Cecil shuffled through the plastic packets, a housewife at market, laying a flat piece on the hot steel deck, sketching. Cecil. His off-duty art he entered every year in the Boardwalk Art Show. Pieces that every year we would help him load home unsold. Last year the judge said that there was a disturbing incompleteness about Cecil's work. The portrait Cecil had done of his girlfriend, Veronica, her in purples and blacks, sitting cross-legged, naked, and headless. Cecil could have just been protecting her modesty or maybe he had not yet mastered faces. Sometimes it seemed Cecil had looked at the wrong thing in a roomful of things to paint. A tennis shoe with a ripped-out tongue. A chair like a step to an open window. Sometimes you would wonder what clues to what crimes we had missed were these things that bubbled up in Cecil's brain. Sometimes somebody who knew Cecil would ask him at the art show if his police work affected his artwork and Cecil would say he didn't really think about it all that much. Cecil would say that the best thing about having his art on display on the boardwalk was that he could sit there all day drinking beer and cultivate snitches from amongst the petty thieves who picked the pockets of the crowds.

Shark parties coming in the inlet from the tournament kicked up wakes where we worked, so Cecil and the police pulled us up for the day. They gave us all who had been in the water with what was left of the girl shots against tetanus and some whiffs of gas-soaked rags for the stench. By the bait shack we hosed ourselves down and waited for the cash handout. Forty dollars a head to flush out the dead girl of our dreams. Later, when some of us drank our money, we had to pick pieces of stenciled flesh we thought we saw from the folds of our clothes. There was nothing they could give us against that. Or against Cecil's suspicion. Empty your pockets before you leave the area, he told us.

Jesus Christ, we said.

Across the inlet boats were flying fin flags, jagged-mouth carcasses bled and lolled across aft decks and were bent over sterns. An Instamatic crowd of tourists in the way of us hustling tips from the beer-drunk fishermen and sunburned mates, us springing lines and running hose. Cecil followed us over, leaning on a gas pump, his sketch-book furled in a back pocket, him just watching.

They had brought in hammerheads and browns, some duskies. Some were cleanly gaffed and dull-eyed, others were beat all to hell, their skin peeled back in places like weather-blistered vinyl. Brain cavities caved in under the gusto of softball bats and lead pipes, shark hunting the thuggery of sport fishing.

All of the boats were in except for our friend Royce and his boat, the *Risky Business*, Royce still outside the inlet dragging a tiger shark backward by the tail to drown it, five miles now and still the shark fought them as they tried to bring it aboard. From the dock you could hear them work the fish over once more, first a shotgun then a service revolver.

A commotion at the weigh-in, the official water people in blue shirts with clipboards and fillet knives were there to gut open shark bellies, part of some research, they said, it was all spelled out in the print at the bottom of the shark-hunt tickets. There were some spit words from the trophy-conscious and a thrown can of beer. Somebody said Cecil ought to step in but Cecil did not.

Royce was finally coming in the inlet, still the occasional gunshot to the head of the monster lashed to his boat. When hoisted up it split a shackled block and broke one of our wrists. Then we winched the shark up on a frame lashed to a telephone pole and nobody could believe it, the fish too large to weigh. The official water people came out of the crowd with all their clipboards and knives and the commotion came up again.

Royce sat up in his flying bridge chewing the strand of monofilament his sunglasses were strung from. Shank, his mate, picked up a gaff off the stern coming around the carcass toward a blue-shirt girl. She had her knife hard into his shark's belly, salt-smelling syrup leaking everywhere.

You had to be careful with Shank, in his mind a bounty hunter of these big fish that he and Royce always won these contests with. His red face eaten up with little skin barnacles, his brain broiled under years of white glare. You could knock Shank down but Shank would get up, and you could knock Shank down again, and again he would get up, until after a while of this you had to pick up some-thing handily substantial like a folding chair to hit him with so he would stay down. You could see this drinking in the Grey Gull afternoons after coming in.

Shank shoved over the official water girl and drew the knife from the shark, spinning it into the telephone pole. Cecil eased out of the crowd and stood close to Shank, whistling admiration at the size of his shark until Shank tapped his gaff, eyes down, against one of his rough raw feet.

What about it, Cecil? said Royce. Royce wanted to know didn't they need a search warrant or something like that to butcher up a trophy fish.

Cecil said it didn't seem so and the water girl went to pull the knife out of the pole but Cecil was there first handing the blade over to Shank, and in that way, everything was all right.

You are always surprised at what is in a shark, some of it still alive coming out, pushing eager flips to show that it is not dead, you looking down thinking, Yeah, right, you've been *eaten!*

In the contest sharks there was the usual, the bluefish, the chunks of tuna heads in onionskin bags that hunters use to work up their slicks of chum. In the tigers you find the bottom dwellers and the sunken throwaway, skates and rays the sharks snuffle off the bottom where they have hidden in the sand. They'll eat rocks, shells, junk. Royce and Shank's shark had other things in it, things like we knew when we saw them spill out would be things that Cecil would want to sketch.

First was the wad of stench that cleared the dock. Then there was a Dixie cup, a beer can, some sheets of undigested skate wings than fanned themselves out like pages in a thumbed-through book. They raked more of the muck until somebody yelled, There's a hand! a scream and a laugh. Cecil stared hard over shoulders while a knife coaxed out the hand. Aw, they said, it's just a rubber glove, faded that water-flesh gray and full of sand. A dog-food can stuck with holes on a string was explained away as what crabbers use to bait their traps. The last was a shark-size bite of plywood and a shotgunned seagull.

It is against our laws to shoot down seagulls to freshen up the chum-slick blood, and that dead bird hurt the way having the winning fish looked, everyone always watching Royce and Shank.

We finished cleaning Royce's boat and helped Shank lug away the shark. Cecil was already drinking beers at the Grey Gull, sketching on a paper sheet torn from his book. He said he was working on getting mouths right. Every time you said anything, Cecil would stare at your mouth as you spoke, making strokes on his page. Having someone stare at your mouth while you talk makes you feel that they do not believe whatever it is you are saying. Cecil had all our mouths down on his paper, working them one by one in little strokes of disbelief.

Royce bought us our beers and picked at Cecil about the dead girl, wasn't she the one twisted up in the tent show, and Cecil said hadn't Royce seen her there himself?

Royce said he'd ever deny being there, and Cecil said, I saw you there that last night with Shank, and Royce said he'd ever deny being there to his wife, and Cecil kept sketching Royce's mouth, saying, Well, I am certainly not your wife.

We all took our turns in disbelief. We had all been to the carnival that last night and we all told our stories. I finally said I didn't like Cecil asking any more dispersions on us and Cecil turned to me saying, Right, and it wasn't you in the bus station that time trying to pick up those runaways with a pocketful of tokens from the video arcade.

I said, That had all been a misundertanding. It had only happened once.

Cecil left us at the Grey Gull, us all sitting around staring at his beer-soggy sketch page, a small wet canvas of little blue kisses.

no more dead girl washed our beach. The inlet was closed for a day while they back-flushed the dredge, not finding anything else, not even a fingernail. There was a short thing in the paper about the girl but the carnival closed and people seemed to forget. The old town lot was empty for a few days except for flattened popcorn boxes and the white crusts of lizard shit, then came the rolling in of the antique cars for our festival. We swept the boardwalk for the art show, stopping on our brooms to watch overhead the flying jets practicing stunts for Sunday.

On Sunday they had the sand-castle contests and the free beer, lifeguard races and the stunt pilots. There were sailors there because the fleet was in, and in the bars there were rounds and rounds of drinks on the houses.

Locals on the boardwalk browsed, the better off from out of town came to buy a certain kind of art for the summer houses. Seascapes, seagulls, sea horses, shipwrecks, sand dunes, and sunsets, all the kind of art you see in the sweep of your flashlight on their walls those nights off-season.

Cecil's work was not what they wanted, wasn't enough sand in it, they said. The boardwalk judge said that Cecil had a hardware-store palette, that when Cecil wanted to do blue sky or blue ocean Cecil just squeezed a tube of blue paint and said Here's blue! The judge said that the best he could say about Cecil's work was that although the paintings were just a menace of fragments, they seemed to have in them a primitive, dreamlike quality. Then the judge looked ahead to the exhibit of seashell wind chimes and sad clown faces on velvet he was to speak on next, Cecil thanking him very much.

By evening we had all dirtied our pockets with money. The light was gone, the beer stands stood empty, spigots blowing foam. Trash drifted along the boardwalk, and on the beach drunks were getting knocked down by knee-high surf.

Cecil. Sitting alone, staring across the boardwalk at his unsold art, beer can adrip from his hand. The last other artist loading a case of turquoise jewelry into a van.

Cecil said that he was glad to see us. I said we had come back over to see if maybe he needed some help taking the exhibition home. I also in secret meant that we might borrow Cecil's car to run an errand to a girl's house by midnight with. You could borrow Cecil's car if you would leave him a note to where it was.

Cecil pointed out to his, the only artwork left on the boardwalk. These are so new I only painted them last night, he said. He said after he had gone to sleep he got up and went into the garage and painted all night. The paint still isn't dry and this morning I got it all over the seats of my car, he said.

You know, when I paint, I don't have any idea what I'm going to paint, Cecil said. Sometimes I see things like

Veronica naked or the sun coming up and I want to paint to capture, and then sometimes I see some piece of something that hangs on the edge of my mind and won't go over and I paint for release. Maybe I should just get myself a camera, Cecil said, and drank his beer.

How much have you had to drink this day? somebody asks Cecil, but Cecil goes on saying into his second six-pack he started to see something *going on* in this new work, a *welling up* on the edge of his mind of a larger picture, something bigger, something all in a series. We all looked to where the paintings were hanging but the sun gone down had emptied them out of everything but the dark.

Cecil stood up and said to allow him to give us a tour of his exhibition. Standing close we looked at the first painting by cigarette-lighter light. Cecil said that the painting was called *S Designs on Gray, What Boat Propeller Looks Like Going Through Skin*, and we all stepped back, Cecil saying he saw it the other day in one of those plastic bags we collected with a number. He said at the police lab downtown that they had told him the girl was still alive when she got the propeller blades across her back. Cecil asked us wasn't it a wonder of modern science?

What made all this well up, said Cecil, is that nobody had a boat out the inlet when the girl disappeared. He had asked us all, hadn't he, Cecil said. S *Designs on Gray*, and it is not for sale.

Cecil showed us next the second picture he said he worked off a sketch he had made shark-hunt day. He said he had liked the look of all the lines and shadows of the workboats tied up near the fuel dock. They cut an angle that caught my eye, Cecil said.

We all took turns holding the lighter to see by until it got too hot to hold and we had to drop it in the sand.

See how this one boat in particular is choked against the dock at low tide? Cecil asked us. We looked but couldn't see, could not have seen that he meant Shank's boat.

Cecil said he had to wonder where the girl got her propeller bites if not in the inlet. He said he also had to wonder why a familiar hand at boats like Shank would cinch his lines too tight in the first place, what, was he in a hurry when he tied up? Cecil said these were the things that hung on the edge of his mind.

Cecil's next work we remembered from seeing in daylight. Cecil had painted a wagon wheel on a piece of raw plywood, then nailed a beaten-flat dog-food can to its hub. He was calling it *Shark Strike!* In the day, pieces of dog food still in the can had attracted flies and people had pointed.

Cecil said he thought the flies added a dimension of motion to the piece.

Cecil said that the key to the work was the monofilament string tied to the dog-food can, like the string that was tied to the can in Royce and Shank's tiger. That fact had hung on his mind, Cecil said, why a crabber would tie string onto a dog-food can he was just going to drop into a crab pot-bait pocket. Cecil said he had never seen that done before.

I was getting anxious about this welling up of Cecil's thought and I wanted to see that girl on an errand by midnight, so I said, Come on, Cecil, do you want us to help take this exhibition home or what?

Cecil said to me that I and all of us were going to sit tight and answer some questions. Cecil said he was going to find out all there was about who killed that girl.

Aw, she drownt in the inlet, somebody said.

Yeah, she fell in, couldn't swim, somebody said.

Likely drunk, fell in and drownt, somebody said.

Dead now, in pieces too, said somebody.

On and on, through and through, dead, over, us we all said.

Cecil said even though she didn't drink and the boyfriend said she could swim he would grant us there was an invitation of death about the girl, the deadness already in her eyes when she danced. Didn't you all see that is what it really was? I saw it, said Cecil. Just like I've seen in so many faces on this beach. I wish I could paint that face. When I see it I know there will be trouble later. That would have rounded out this little exhibition of mine, Cecil said, a painting of the fear on your faces from her invitation. I saw all of you feeding off her that last night and I knew there would be trouble. I wish I could paint that hunger for the fear but I haven't mastered faces yet. Your hunger! Your fear! said Cecil suddenly, staggering up toward us. You all know I'm right, he said.

Steady, Cecil, we said. You've been drinking.

Yes, I have, said Cecil and he sat down.

But I've seen something here, he said, something welling up in the edges of these paintings. I don't have anything on any one of you specific but I got it all in general. Somebody coaxed her out on the ocean then ran over her with his boat. Her body just came through the inlet on the tide.

Nobody could have got that woman to do nothing she didn't want to do, we said, and Cecil said, Somebody made her an unusual offer, something she had never heard before to do. It wouldn't have been for a man or a drink or anything else. Somebody with a load of chum offered to take her out in the ocean and feed the animals. Somebody asked her would she like to feed the biggest fishes ever.

That's crazy, we said. Nobody goes out in the ocean in the middle of the night to feed fish.

Oh, but Cecil said, feeding the animals was the only thing she had ever seemed to like to do.

Cecil rapped his knuckles on his plywood painting. Digging out the plywood like the piece they found in Royce and Shank's shark, Cecil said he finally found an old piece to paint on in his garage. Holding it he remembered a trick he had seen fishing one time, a man opening the Sunday paper page by page and laying it out over the ocean, the man saying the fish liked the shade when it was hot and would congregate. Cecil said the man told him professionals sometimes used baited plywood but it was a lot of trouble.

So what, we said.

So what does Shank do off-season, Cecil asked us and we all knew, us all during hurricane season for a few dollars each riding crew with Shank in his truck nailing plywood over cottage windows on the south of the beach.

So what, we said.

So the night before the shark hunt Shank goes out to

rig the contest laying out plywood baited with dog-food cans and chum. All he would have to do then is figure out the current the next day to find all the big fish congregating in the shade.

Your figuring sounds fishy, somebody said.

Fishy, Cecil said, is Shank's workboat snugged too tight to the dock shark-hunt day. It means to me that when Shank tied up his boat there was something big on his sunburnt mind, something so big that after all these years tying up tide in and tide out, something made him forget to rightly rig his rig.

Rig his rig? You're drunk, Cecil, we said.

I think this is more asking dispersions, I said to Cecil. I said that since he was leaning so hard on Shank why didn't he ask Shank about all of this instead of fouling us up in it, and Cecil said that nobody can seem to find Shank, wherever he has conveniently disappeared off to, from Panama to New Brunswick. I'll tell you why you are all fouled up in this, is because I asked you all, Did any boats go in or out the night before we found the girl, and everybody said, Oh no, nobody went out at all, and the only reason beside my sketch of the lines I figured it was Shank was by checking all the gas receipts at the pump house and I saw he'd had to top off his tanks to lay bait and rig the contest. But none of you all saw fit to help me out because you all are so tight with Royce and Shank, everybody wanting Royce and Shank to be able to bring in the biggest shark no matter how they get it so you all can clean up Royce's boat and gut Shank's shark to put in your pockets a little extra spending money. Nobody is going to worry if somehow this girl they saw in the way they saw her got herself out in the ocean with Shank and into some trouble she couldn't handle where something happened, she was pushed or jumped and Shank ran over her with his boat. That's still murder. That is still murder. That's you helping decide to write that girl out of the life book and you all can hardly make the decision of whether to bathe or not, much less that one. You all keep quiet because everybody here likes to feed off Royce and Shank, never mind there was murder.

And I'll tell you something else. I think it takes more than one man to handle those plywood and dog-food rigs over the side of a workboat, and I don't think Shank was by himself, especially if he could get a little help for cheap, a little help maybe for a little pocket money for somebody to go off and drink on and run around to get their goddamn errands done by midnight!

I said, That does it. We said we didn't want to borrow

his goddamn car anymore. We said we just wanted to help him move his goddamn no-sale exhibit home. And Cecil said we were all going to help him move the exhibition all right. He said he was going to give us all a little piece of it to take home whatever rat-hole or sewer pipe we slept in calling home was. He said he wanted us to get us a hammer and get us a nail, and to nail up on the walls of our rat-holes and sewer pipes the piece he was going to give to each of us, he wanted each of us every time we woke up from our cheap-help-drinking sleep to think about being in on writing somebody out of the life book, that if we thought we could sanely think about hiding fear by helping hide the man who killed the girl, well then we ought to have some lovely artwork of our own of the whole thing to help us contemplate with.

Cecil ripped down all his art and pushed it on us, a piece to us all.

Cecil, we said.

Go on with it, get out of here, Cecil said. Each of you gets a piece. Any more than one piece, I can tell you, is too much for one man to bear.

Cecil, we said.

Go, said Cecil. Scurry to your rat-holes and sewer

pipes. I don't ever want to see your faces. And don't leave town, ever!

We all took our art. There wasn't the best of us there who could tell Cecil what we knew, how wrong he was about us. Men like us can never tell a man like Cecil all we know. We could never tell him of a place we knew, a place where finally the ocean is blue blue, the eelgrass is green green, where a man like Shank might rest forever, wrapped in chains to keep him down, his flesh feeding the fishes and no more murder in his crab-eaten eyes. We could never tell a man like Cecil about a pretty place like that. But maybe we hoped as we scattered with what he had given us in our arms, maybe someday somebody could paint him a picture.

the birds
for christmas

We wanted *The Birds* for Christmas. We had seen the commercials for it on the television donated thirdhand by the Merchant Seamen's and Sailors' Rest Home, a big black-and-white Zenith of cracked plastic and no knobs, a dime stuck in the channel selector. You could adjust the picture and have no sound, or hi-fi sound and no picture. We just wanted the picture. We wanted to see *The Birds*.

The Old Head Nurse said not to get our hopes up. It was a "Late Show" after Lights Out the night before Christmas Eve. She said it would wake the babies and scare the Little Boys down on the far end of the ward. Besides, she said, she didn't think it was the type of movie we should be seeing Christmas week.

She said she was certain there would be Rudolph and Frosty on. That would be more appropriate for us to watch on the night before Christmas Eve.

"*Fuck* Frosty," Michael Christian said to me. "I see that a *hunrett* times. I want to see *The Birds*, man. I want to see those birds get all up *in* them people's hair. That's some real Christmas TV to me."

Michael Christian and I were some of the last Big Boys to be claimed for Christmas. We were certain *someone* would eventually come for us. We were not frightened yet. There were still some other Big Boys around—the Big Boy who ran away to a gas station every other night, the Human Skeleton who would bite you, and the guy locked away on the sun porch who the Young Doctors were taking apart an arm and a leg at a time.

The Young Doctors told Michael Christian that their Christmas gift to him would be that one day he would be able to do a split onstage like his idol, James Brown. There never seemed to be any doubt in Michael Christian's mind about that. For now, he just wanted to see *The Birds* while he pretended to be James Brown in the Hospital.

Pretending to be James Brown in the Hospital was not without its hazards for Michael Christian; he had to remember to keep his head lifted from his pillow so as not to *bedhead* his budding Afro. Once, when he was practicing his singing, the nurses rushed to his bed asking him where it hurt.

"I'm warming up 'I Feel Good,' stupid bitches," said Michael Christian. Then his bed was jerked from the wall and wheeled with great speed, pushed and pulled along by hissing nurses, jarring other bedsteads, Michael Christian's wrists hanging over the safety bedrails like jailhouse-window hands; he was on his way to spend a couple of solitary hours out in the long, dark, and empty hall, him rolling his eyes at me as he sped past, saying, "Aw, man, now I feel BAD!"

Bed wheeling into the hall was one of the few alternatives to corporal punishment the nurses had, most of them being reluctant to spank a child in traction for spitting an orange pip at his neighbor, or to beat a completely burned child for cursing. Bed wheeling into the hall was especially effective at Christmastime, when it carried the possibility of missing Christmas programs. A veteran of several Christmases in the Hospital and well acquainted with the grim Christmas programs, Michael Christian scoffed at the treasures handed out by the church and state charities—the aging fruit, the surplus ballpoint pens, the occasional batches of recycled toys that didn't work, the games and puzzles with missing pieces. Michael Christian's Christmas Wish was as specific as mine. I wanted a miniature train set with batteries so I could lay out the track to run around on my bed over the covers. Not the big Lionel size or the HO size. I wanted the set you could see in magazines, where they show you the actual size of the railroad engine as being no larger than a walnut.

"You never get that, man," Michael Christian said, and he was right.

James Brown in the Hospital's Christmas Wish was for *The Birds* for Christmas. And, as Michael Christian's friend, I became an accomplice in his desire. In that way, "birds" became a code, the way words can among boys.

"Gimme some BIRDS!" Michael Christian would squawk when the society ladies on their annual Christmas visit asked us what we wanted.

"How about a nice hairbrush?" a society lady said, laying one for white people at the foot of Michael Christian's bed.

"I want a pick," Michael Christian told her.

"A pick? A shovel and a pick? To dig with?" asked the society lady.

"I think he wants a comb for his hair," I said. "For his Afro."

"That's right: a pick," said Michael Christian. "Tell this stupid white bitch something. *Squawk, squawk,*" he said, flapping his elbows like wings, as the nurses wheeled him out into the hall. "Gimme some BIRDS!" he shouted, and when they asked me, I said to give me some birds, too.

Michael Christian's boldness over the Christmas programs increased when Ben, the night porter, broke the television. Looking back, it may not be fair to say that Ben, the night porter, actually broke the television, but one evening it was soundlessly playing some kiddie Christmas show and Ben was standing near it mopping up a spilt urinal can when the screen and the hope of Michael Christian's getting his Christmas Wish blackened simultaneously. Apologetic at first, knowing what even a soundless television meant to children who had rarely seen any television at all, Ben then offered to "burn up your butt, Michael Christian, legs braces and all" when Michael Christian hissed "stupid nigger" at Ben, beneath the night nurse's hearing. It was a somber Lights Out.

The next night, a priest and some students from the seminary came by. Practice Preachers, Michael Christian said. While one of the students read the Christmas story from the Bible, Michael Christian pretended to peck his own eyes out with pinched fingers. When the story was finished, Michael Christian said, "Now, you say the sheep-herding guys was so afraid, right?"

"*Sore* afraid," said the Practice Preacher. "The shep-herds had never seen angels before, and they were *sore* afraid."

"Naw," said Michael Christian. "I'll tell you what—they saw these big white things flapping down and they was big *birds*, man. I know *birds*, man, I know when you got bird *problems*, man."

"They were *angels*," said the young seminary student.

"Naw," said Michael Christian. "They was big white birds, and the sheepherding guys were *so* afraid the big white birds was swooping down and getting all up in they *hair* and stuff! *Squawk, squawk!*" he said, flapping around in his bed.

"*Squawk, squawk!*" I answered, and two of the Practice Preachers assisted the nurses in wheeling Michael Christian into the hall and me into the linen cupboard.

One night in the week before Christmas, a man named Sammy came to visit. He had been a patient as a child, and his botched cleft-palate and harelip repairs were barely concealed by a weird line of blond mustache. Sammy owned a hauling company now, and he showed up blistering drunk, wearing a ratty Santa suit, and began handing out black-strapped Timex Junior wristwatches. I still have mine, somewhere.

One by one we told Sammy what we wanted for Christmas, even though we were not sure, because of his speech defect, that that was what he was asking. Me, the walnut train; Michael Christian, *The Birds*. We answered without enthusiasm, without hope: it was all by rote. By the end of the visit, Sammy was a blubbering sentimental mess, reeking of alcohol and promises. Ben, the night porter, put him out.

it was Christmas Eve week. The boy who kept running away finally ran away for good. Before he left, he snatched the dime from the channel selector on our broken TV. We all saw him do it and we didn't care. We didn't even yell out to the night nurse, so he could get a better head start than usual.

It was Christmas Eve week, and Michael Christian lay listless in his bed. We watched the Big Boy ward empty. Somebody even came for one of the moaners, and the guy out on the sun porch was sent upstairs for a final visit to the Young Doctors so they could finish taking him apart.

On the night before Christmas Eve, Michael Christian and I heard street shoes clicking down the long corridor that led to where we lay. It was after Lights Out. We watched and waited and waited. It was just Sammy the Santa, except this time he was wearing a pale-blue leisure suit, his hair was oiled back, and his hands, holding a red-wrapped box, were clean.

What we did not want for Christmas were wristwatches. What we did not want for Christmas were bars of soap. We did not want any more candy canes, bookmarks, ballpoint pens, or somebody else's last year's broken toy. For Christmas we did not want plastic crosses, dot books, or fruit baskets. No more handshakes, head pats, or storybook times. It was the night before Christmas Eve, and Michael Christian had not mentioned *The Birds* in days, and I had given up on the walnut train. We did not want any more Christmas Wishes.

Sammy spoke with the night nurse, we heard him plead that it was Christmas, and she said all right, and by her flashlight she brought him to us. In the yellow spread of her weak batteries, we watched Michael Christian unwrap a portable television.

There was nothing to be done except plug the television into the wall. It was Christmas, Sammy coaxed the

45

reluctant night nurse. They put the little TV on a chair, and we watched the end of an Andy Williams Christmas Special. We watched the eleven-o'clock news. Then the movie began: *The Birds*. It was Christmas, Sammy convinced the night nurse.

The night nurse wheeled her chair away from the chart table and rolled it to the television set. The volume was low, so as not to disturb the damaged babies at the Little Boy end of the ward—babies largely uncollected until after the holidays, if at all. Sammy sat on an empty bed. He patted it. Michael Christian and I watched *The Birds*.

During the commercials, the night nurse checked the hall for the supervisor. Sammy helped her turn any infant that cried out. The night nurse let Sammy have some extra pillows. Michael Christian spoke to me only once during a commercial when we were alone, he said, "Those birds messing them people *up*."

When the movie was over, it was the first hours of Christmas Eve. The night nurse woke Sammy and let him out through the sun porch. She told us to go to sleep, and rolled her chair back to her chart table. In the emptiness you could hear the metal charts click and scratch, her folds of white starch rustle. Through a hole in the pony blanket I had pulled over my head I could see Michael Christian's bed. His precious Afro head was buried deep beneath his pillow.

At the dark end of the ward a baby cried in its sleep and then was still.

It was Christmas Eve, and we were sore afraid.

fun at the beach

Got a letter from a girl said we ought to get together before her husband gets parole. Said maybe we could rent another bungalow down at Big Bill's Beach Cabanas like last time, maybe steam up some shrimp and suck out the heads, maybe break a box of old 45s against the walls again, the tequila-drinking things, things like me doing it to her from behind with her leaning out the bungalow window whistling at sailors on the boardwalk, what did I think?

I wrote back and said, Do I know you?

Got a letter back said she's got a big car now, a '72 Caprice with a four-hundred engine that runs hot, no AC but a backseat that could fuck four. Said the big-engine car could make the four-hour trip under three, she can get off early because she quit her job. Said she wants to run the big car out on the beach and get it stuck in deep sand, stuck in so deep it doesn't come out, and then us doing it in the backseat until the tide comes in the windows pouring over us doing it.

I wrote back and said, You never told me you were married.

I get a card back with it written in that sort of teenage scrawl all over it that she wants me to shoot in her front, back, top, bottom, in her ear, and in the pocket of her white-satin slicker. Said she wants to squeeze out the last drop after all the shooting and for me to drink oyster water and pineapple juice to get ready, one for the salt and one for the sweet, when would be a good weekend?

I wrote back and said, What's he been in prison for?

I get back a smeary, hand-crumpled piece of paper with two tiny twisted hairs stuck to it. I leave the whole matter alone, not hearing a word more, me just lying around on my back-porch chaise lounge with my toxic memory, watching squall lines build out at sea. Then my telephone rings. It's her. She's at Lloyd's Auto Theft Store six blocks from where I live, saying she's already in town, her husband's already got the parole, do I mind when she comes him sleeping on the floor?

My memory won't open for me to stir it up to find out who this girl is. She signs her name with a big *S* or a *P* or a *D* and puts a smiley face over what I guess is an *i* at the end of her name. I've taken a few girls from out of town down to Big Bill's Beach Cabanas for a few days of fun with drink and an effort or two at a poke, but in those whiskey-dick days I mostly had to thumb it in or use Popsicle sticks and duct tape. I doubt that part about me doing it to her from behind while she whistled at sailors, unless she was the one who used to get me all worked up talking dirty about Christmas pudding and hairless cats.

And her husband on the floor. I've tangled with a few husbands before, I've got the weird hair-part and brain damage to prove it. My floor is a special place I have in the past shared with my dog, Bo. Crawling home on all fours like I used to, badly sotted so as not able to lift myself to bed but better than being able to stand up and lurch forward and possibly piss in my sock drawer for the hundredth time. Bo often takes the space on the floor between the porch and the bathroom, where there is sometimes a wing of breeze and where he is certain to be a foot obstacle contributing to any injury I can receive tripping over him in my nightly dark stumbles. In my bottle-in-front-of-me-frontal-lobotomy days I never fed Bo all that much, him not liking that radium-enriched crushed-chicken-beak-and-crab-shell mix I used to buy him. So when he'd whine in hunger I'd just throw open the door, splashing my Ny-Quil-and-spot-of-tonic cocktail, and tell him to just go on out and kill something. Bo is fat now from the pizza crusts he tips from trash cans along the Touron Strip. His breath is often of onion and anchovy. I am certain that Bo's general poor disposition comes from having to forage, and having been struck by so many out-of-town touron cars on vacation. I think he suffers the same bone languors and achy joints as a bone-ruined boozer like myself does when the weather changes and the squall lines build out at sea.

When I get the call from the girl down at Lloyd's Auto Theft Store I have strong thoughts that excite me greatly. I have a thought of Bo bounding down from the wild sand dunes next door and eating the girl and her convict husband as they step from her new big car. In my thought they have pushed down the locks before getting out and now they can't get back in and Bo eats them so that he is full for three months and I have a car to drive.

Here is where my memory serves to deflate my thinking. I remember I am the only person Bo has ever bounded over the dunes to eat. That was when I had a job and would come home in my checkerboard sport coat and monkey pants after a hard day as a cardboard technician and Bo would come ripsnarling through the sand around the downstairs shower stall, maybe pausing to gulp a frog Buddha-like beneath the foot-wash faucet. Bo would pretend not to recognize me until he'd drawn some saber-toothed slices of meat from my ankles.

My fantasy was ultimately deflating as I heard a big-engine car pull up outside and doors close, footsteps up the stairs. I pulled up my pants and got off the plastic chaise lounge.

We shook hands around the girl, her saying I'm me and he's the E-man, remember? and I say No, I don't, and he says Hey, no hard feelings, and I say That's likely.

He wasn't so big, about my size, his hands were smooth so I thought maybe Safecracker until he smiled and I saw his bright teeth filed into points. He rubbed his temples and said You were thinking maybe Safecracker. Then he asked if he might borrow the ten dollars I had wadded in my front right pants pocket. I gave it to him and the E-man went out the door to the street. I asked the girl Can he always do that? and she said Yes, he's pretty good at borrowing money from strange people.

As I listened to the girl, a sphere of swamp-gas memory bubbled up in the stagnant slime of my mind, it bubbled up as a fox-fire haint of recollection that told me this girl had an extra nipple on her chest and could bend a quarter in half. I knew it was a trick but I remembered liking to see her do it.

We ought to get straight on this visit and the husband, I said, and the girl said what she ought to do is lie down, just lie down. She said her mind chattered with polarity static.

I asked her if the E-man was some sort of psychic menace. Oh no, I said, he's not the Party Magician Killer, is he?

The girl ignored me and crackled down on my split plastic chaise lounge, the one with mites and tiny sand spiders that leave red pox on your neck and face if you sleep out there on the porch all night. The girl started jittering asleep, her fits pulling fibers of spun packing material from my brain, and I remembered her then, I remembered these bedtime thrashings that she had once told me were the flashbacks from doing a mixing bowl of hog tranquilizer as a child. I remembered sleeping with this girl. I remembered sleeping with her was like sleeping with a fistfight.

She was about thirty minutes into REM sleep, beating herself in the face and lurching all around on the chaise lounge. I watched her from a safe distance sitting on my croquet set. Down on the beach The Boys were passing, beachcombing for nickel-deposit cans and bathing-suit change. They stopped and looked up at us on the porch. Put a spoon in her mouth, one of them suggested. Thanks, I said. Say, said one, is that the E-man's wife you're fooling around with again? What do you know about the E-man, I asked down, but The Boys took flight and roosted in the wild sand dunes just down from my house. No E-man, not that, the girl said in her wrestle with sleep on my chaise.

The E-man came back carrying a big bag from the Subdollar Discount Store, wearing dollar shorts with this donkey dong dangling out the bottom. He's wearing a ninety-nine-cent T-shirt that says BEACHIN' BABY, black-and-orange flip-flops clap around his feet. You should see what I got, he said, banging the big bag up the steps.

The E-man's black-and-orange flip-flops catch in the screen door and he's swinging his loot around trying to free himself, like a seaside trick-or-treating apparition. He dumps his bag on the table. The E-man has a new plastic duck camera with duck beaks on the side and a blue plastic carrying case with a duck head on the front. His shorts pockets are full of film. He says he left his old clothes in the ladies' room at Lloyd's Auto Theft Store, the men's room was locked with someone grunting inside. The E-man looked different to me. There is a flattened tube of hair rinse in the Subdollar bag. His previously blond scruff is now the black coffee color of mine.

In the bottom of the bag I see a set of Revlon files and a pair of gravity boots. From my ten dollars the E-man gives me back my change, one hundred and seventy-six dollars and forty-five cents.

Hey, come on out and take my picture, the E-man says, barefoot and dong dangling out the back door to the beach. The slap of the screen didn't move the girl snoring in fits, drooling on the swan-cupped wrist tucked beneath her cheek. I set a box fan down beside her to blow off the fat mosquitoes that took flight in the dead air, the squall line stalled and upended on the horizon.

I burned up three rolls of film on the E-man splashing around in our oily surf. At night, kerosene tankers flush their bilges offshore. You wake up with a ball-peen-hammer headache and a taste for a six-pack of Sterno. A crystal-meth crowd came through where we were taking pictures, throwing sand in one another's eyes. I took several pictures of the E-man with his arm around a girl, her hair the color of fiberglass insulation. She peeled back the E-man's lips to better see his filed teeth. Bite me, she said. The E-man's bites left hoofprints of puncture that bled well when the fiberglass girl pinched them. The fiberglass girl got the E-man to bite all of her friends and he chewed on their arms, their ankles, their necks. The whole crystal-meth party set off down the beach again, clearing bathers out of the water with stories of biting fish, their arms and legs held forth in evidence.

The E-man wanted to go home. He was shivering. I was shivering, too, thinking I was in need of a drink. The E-man sucked the crystal-meth blood from his BEACHIN' BABY T-shirt. I was thinking about heading us over to where The Boys were sitting in the storm drain beneath Sixty-eighth Street. Nothing fancy, some malt lager cut with high-school-stolen formaldehyde, some seaweed cigarettes, the idiot strumming show tunes on a rubber-band cigar-box guitar. The usual.

The E-man was adamant about getting home before dark. He said he needed to do his spinal exercises. We walked along beneath the boardwalk and the E-man began to shrink. His blue duck-head camera bounced against his caved-in breastbone. He was so bent over, his small face closing up. He was bent so that he waddled when he walked, his wrists flopped, and a hand of his found a hand of mine. A touron on the boardwalk said to its mother Look, man, that guy is walking a monkey! Cheetah, hey Cheetah! You fucker!

The E-man was so shrunk up by the time we got to my house that I could have easily balled him up in my hands and drop-kicked him onto the deck of the kerosene tanker idling along, eyeballing our shore.

officer welt came by the next morning. Officer Welt survived his stroke but stutters, and sometimes his hands begin to shake and his billy club clatters to the sidewalk during a pressure-point interrogation of a perpetrator. In these glassy-eyed lapses of serving and protecting, an arm from an accomplice in the crowd will reach in and jostle the perpetrator into action. Run, fool, the accomplice will say.

The warrant against me was written in red ballpoint pen in the margins of a take-out menu from Ninja Assassin over on the good end of Baltic. Apparently, the charges were Unlawful Assembly with a Chimpanzee and Harboring a Dog. I tipped Officer Welt a couple of bucks and latched the screen. The chucklehead sharpsters in the police car parked at the curb laughed and slapped the dashboard, then bumped the siren a couple of times to clue Officer Welt. Officer Welt had addled over into the dunes near the house. Last month the sharpsters put Officer Welt out in the intersection of where Pristine merges with Blowmouth Expressway to direct rush-hour touron traffic. A bunch of people lost teeth in officiously dispatched and orchestrated head-ons.

I went into the kitchen and fried up some green tomato slices and a half dozen eggs dated Armed Forces Day. I set the platter on the table and went out on the porch to get the girl off the rotted chaise lounge where she spent the night. I myself slept with a croquet mallet in the covers and a tenpenny nail beneath my pillow. All night long the E-man was hanging upside down in the shower, singing, his gravity boots hooked into the plumbing, doing his spinal stretches, singing, singing in the running water long after I knew the hot had run out. I clutched my mallet and gnawed on my nail.

I got the girl up off the chaise lounge, her neck a red poisoned spotting of bitten pox.

Out on the beach the E-man had built a high-walled castle surrounded by a tidally fed moat. I came out and E-man pointed out the stockade, the suborbital module recovery unit, the library, the Hall of Kings, and the microwave towers he has built stacking sand with my bait bucket. Hey, take my picture, he says. After breakfast, I say.

I pulled the plug on the hot plate of Styrofoam coffee and poured it all around. The girl had both hands around her cup, letting her eggs go cold. The E-man was elbow into his eggs with a Navy soup spoon I used to use to turn GroDog out of the can for Bo when Bo would eat that radioactive feed. The E-man licked his plate, hunkered over it like Bo hunkered over fresh roadkill, the E-man gnawing a little on the ceramic edge, a little, to fight tartar buildup, he said.

By the time I sat down the E-man was into the girl's breakfast, her eggs, her tomatoes, then he ate the platter of half a loaf of freezer toast. Back to work, he says, shaking sand out of his new black hair onto his plate. The clothes of mine he stole out of my room while I was with Officer

Welt, my favorite COONASS shirt and my merchant-marine trousers, seem to fit him nicely. It could have easily been me I was watching putting his dish in the rubber tray I have for a sink and setting off out the back door to forearm some sand against the seaward castle wall. The incoming tide was threatening the boutique.

You and me gotta talk, I said to the girl.

All right, she says, I've had my coffee. She drops off her dress, naked. She peels my two cold fried eggs off my plate. She pulls them to her breasts until the yellow parts break soaping between her knuckles. She moves nearer, leading into me, dripping yellow until we are an egg sandwich on the floor in front of the stove.

I am trying but I can't do it. I hold my breath to hear footsteps across the sand. Her breath is deader than stale squall, the tiny bites, pinheads of fester on her neck.

Somebody is on the back steps!

The back door slams before I can pitch off. There is the knife on the counter I used to make the tomato slices. There is the shard of two-by-four by the door I used to prop the shutter. There is the nine-millimeter Glock pistol in the pulled-open tinfoil drawer. Everything is closer to whoever makes doorfall first.

Shadow in the doorway. My back winces waiting for

tomato knife or pistol shot. Instead, in comes Bo, clicking across the linoleum. I growl at him and Bo growls at me. I can see he's been tipping cans down on Thirty-second, behind the Vegetarian Vagabond, bean-pizza crust and organic sauce stuck in his uppers and canines.

I get up off the sandwich, take my Styrofoam coffee out on the porch. The E-man is undertaking a major excavation near the castle. I look back into the kitchen. The girl is sitting on the floor, her back wading into the warmth of the oven left on for freezer toast. Her eyes are closed, Bo licks the broken yellow off her naked breasts.

In the evening we have a wind. It blows and blows. Offshore, the kerosene tankers put out their heavy sea anchors; in town, trash cans tip of their own accord, Bo no doubt in on the feast. The wind scours the E-man castle and pushes the dunes' footing under my house. Where people have used the dunes for a pet cemetery, the wind uncovers bones and fur and collars. Ashes to ashes, the people sometimes say, standing on the tall dune at night, winding up the slingshot of old beach towel with Little Precious stiff inside before flinging the parcel into the gritty abyss.

The wind also herded The Boys around my pilings downstairs, passing around a restaurant jar of fermented cocktail onions. The idiot had brought his rubber-band cigar-box guitar to accompany the E-man hanging upside down in the shower, hanging upside down there with that infernal singing. The girl didn't seem to hear it. She was jerking around asleep sitting at the kitchen table, her deck of fifty-one solitaire blown all over the house by the wind.

That infernal singing.

I smashed a lamp with my croquet mallet. I covered my ears.

I took the keys to the girl's car and chased The Boys out from under the house. The shower stall was empty, the cold water dribbled into the drain. I started the car, the moon was a drip on the dark hood. I had decided to go bowling and blame it on the E-man when the police came. I drove up the north end of the beach and bowled over some lawn furniture and chased some children playing kick-the-can screaming across their yards. I ran over their bicycles and toys. I headed down Diablo Pass and bowled over some new chain-link and flattened a picket fence. The girl had been right, there's nothing like a great big car with a four-hundred engine and 170 horses under the hood.

On Shore Drive I bowled through a section of high-way barricades where they are completing the I-4 inter-change, and I sideswiped a school bus of children coming

home from Bible camp. For good measure in the home-
stretch I bowled over every trash can from Seventy-
seventh to Twelfth, even catching one that hung stuck
under the car spreading friction sparks down the boulevard
as I drug it along. The sparks jumped tourons off the side-
walks and set a small trash fire on the corner of Beulah and
Dike. It was a small fire when The Boys happened upon it,
but they tended it all night with siding they stripped from
the Pentecoastal Amphibian Youth Hostel, themselves
nursing an economy-size bottle of flame retardant. At
home, I slipped the keys to the car back into the girl's
purse and lay in bed with my croquet mallet and my tenpenny nail.

The E-man was nowhere around.

In the morning the police sharpsters hacked their way
through my screen door with machetes, two hysterical
tourons in tow. I was just going to point out where they
could find the perpetrator of the previous night's driving
atrocities, out playing in the sand on the beach, when the
touron woman screamed That's the monster! The touron
couple were shouting and pointing at me, ace bandages and
bloody gauze around their necks. Look at what that filthy
beast did to me, the woman said, unwinding a bit of gauze
to show some very distinctive E-man teeth bites. Before I

could raise an argument in my defense a police sharpster knocked me unconscious with a fire extinguisher. They let Officer Welt inch me into the back of the police car using a come-along winch and a length of piano wire.

When I came to, handcuffed behind my back in the car, I was informed I was being charged with Unlawful Digging of Tiger Traps on the Beach. The touron couple had been taking a midnight stroll by my house breathing in the kerosene and had fallen into a carefully concealed covered hole where someone about my size had tried to eat them starting with their necks. The couple fought the sandpit monster off with a wine bottle and the woman's shoes, and saw the monster run into my house wearing a shirt that said COONASS on it. The man touron had managed to rip a shank of coffee-black hair from the perpetrator's head. Could I account for every hair on my head last night?

I said I'd been out bowling and they said Likely.

Every time I opened my mouth in my own defense the police sharpsters would speed up and then slam on the brakes, shouting, Look out for that dog! and I would go crashing handcuffed face-first into the steel chicken-wire between the seats. It was great fun for the sharpsters. As we turned onto Briarwood Lane, Bo came skipping out from behind the Megadeath Deli and the police cruiser jumped the curb to send him pinwheeling into a stand of rental bicycles.

Hey, I shouted, that was my dog! Dog! shouted the police sharpsters and they slammed on the brakes.

The tiger-trap rap was a basic no-brainer, twelve hours in the cooler and fifty-dollar fine. I was home for breakfast, Armed Forces eggs and Styrofoam coffee. The E-man had filled in his tiger trap and now was populating his sea-walled city with stick people made from the bones of pets he found in the dunes next door. The radio was on in my room, the door was closed, I could hear the girl talking and Bo whimpering inside. I kicked the door open like I had done a long time ago and my memory slipped its poison in my mind again. Inside the room the girl was tending Bo's broken leg with plaster and liniment and when she looked at me like she looked at me when I kicked in the door I knew at once that once I had loved her and that it had been a very long time ago.

I went out on the beach and kicked sand in the E-man's face. How dare you come back around here, I said. I kept kicking sand on him covering him with sand but he began to shrink up. Oh no you don't, I said, you're not going to shrink on me. I was trying to stretch him out when he began to sing. Stop it! I said but he kept on singing until I was paralyzed by one single note and a need for a drink.

i woke up the next morning side-faced in the sand on the beach. Just before I awoke I was dreaming I was trying to spit a note through an open window in my house to the girl I am certain I once loved, but the police sharpsters were pulling out my tongue with needle-nosed pliers. I snored myself awake, kind of coughed, and opened my eyes in time to see a hermit crab scuttle out of my gaping mouth across the sand.

I sat up. There was a black crater in front of my house like a garbage meteor had struck, and my memory lurched a gear, then stuck, and I remembered The Boys and the jubilant dancing, our jubilant dancing around a fire, swilling and passing around gallons of cleaning products. The fire. It had been the E-man's sea-walled city with a flood tide of kerosene trapped in his moats. Someone. Someone had lit it. For hours burned the boutique and the library, the Hall of Kings, the bone people trapped in the church and burned to crematorium bucket cinders.

I hesitated to run my tongue across my teeth, knowing that each missing tooth and loose molar represented an attempt at pavement-gnawing or a curbside chew, or some justifiably outraged citizen's well-swung pool cue. My tongue made a quick sweep from cheek to cheek and I neatly sliced it open on my front teeth that had been overnight filed into razored points.

Marching to the house, I overheard my bellyful of industrial shirt-and-slacks solvent sloshing around in the rinse cycle of my stomach. Of course Bo was gone. Of course the girl was gone. Of course the car had left the driveway. But I heard the water running in the downstairs shower. I could see the heels of gravity boots hung in the underside of my downstairs plumbing. I flung open the door to the shower stall. The E-man was still there. He was hanging upside down in the running water, a tenpenny nail driven through his shrunken heart with a croquet mallet.

the boys come to visit me on special days. They bring me doggie chews for my teeth and news from the outside. Sometimes they bring me photographs they have taken with the duck-head camera. They always have pictures of the girl and Bo. The girl and Bo have settled into my house, living nicely there. The Boys show me photographs of the girl and Bo on the beach in the kerosene evenings, her throwing blackened bones from the castle fire for him to fetch. They show me these photos but they don't let me keep them.

That's all right.

Just the other day I got a letter from the girl. It said Thank you thank you thank you. When I get out of here I plan to resettle in with her and the dog, kind of like old times. If memory serves, we will be very, very happy.

charming ɪ bɾ, fɾ. dɾ. wndws, quiet, safe. fee.

Insomnia is easy.

When you get insomnia, you open the french door windows to the apartment you can't afford and sight down on the riffraff on the corner selling drugs with your loaded .38 Smith & Wesson Airweight, and squeeze on the trigger just enough to scare yourself; or you call the pay phone they are all standing around and make vicious remarks from your dark perch about their appearance, their clothes, their grooming, the way they grab their dicks; or you can fill condoms with water and sling them at the drunken gangster patrons of the pasta place diagonally under your apartment as they come out screaming,

screaming some boisterous gangster rubbish, knotting up their ties in cheap gangster fashion, shadow-boxing the terrified immaculate Chilean parking-garage attendant next door to the gangster pasta place, the way they straighten his tie too tight, lifting him from his green plastic chair, sending him off to fetch their Buick, two of the drunken gangster guys wrapping themselves in the long garage-door chains, breathing to break them across their chests, chewing the links in their mouths, growling gladiators chained to fight bears while a third gangster turns on the garden hose the immaculate Chilean uses to wash the piss and vomit of previous gangster patrons off the sidewalk, the third gangster spraying passing cars with the hose, daring them to stop, crouching between parked cars he hoses down a passing couple, unarmed people who dare not turn and face six or seven drunken gangster guys, and then, in insomnia, you, you lean out naked and swing the water-gorged reservoir-tipped and tied-off latex condom a couple of times out the french door windows of the apartment you cannot afford, you swing the condom back and forth, building trajectory, then you let it go and peek while it sails upward spastically like a happy fat girl's breasts bubbling in the top of her cheap low-cut cotton summer dress as she laughs bouncing high-heeled down subway steps, charming 1 br, fr. dr. wndws, quiet, safe. ree.

you marveling at the wonderful dynamics of these dualities, the elasticity, the abundance, the constraint, this vulgar water-stretched latex mockery with its reservoir-tip nipple sails high over the sidewalk then begins its descent, and it doesn't strike the gangster with the hose, or the two playing Spartacus in the chains, it doesn't actually strike any of the gangsters, it explodes on the sidewalk sopping the Big Man Gangster's shoes and cuffs, sending the gangsters suddenly looking up, looking up, looking up not seeing anything up there, dropping the hose, shrugging off the chains, shouting at each other, the Big Man Gangster calm but seething, one of the little gangsters mopping the Big Man's shoes with a handkerchief, Sorry sorry sorry boss, the Big Man having tolerated the drunken child's play now finds himself surrounded by *idiots*, pistol-packing *idiots* supposed to dive in front of the don to take slugs can't even take a water balloon, and one of the gangster brutes, to do *something*, examines the water on the pavement, looking for clues to the guy we're going to get for doing this, Big Don, Boss, yeah, he taps around in the water pattern on the sidewalk *sensing* the water pattern, something to tell him, because he's a microsecond from pulling out his B.O. Plenty TEC nine on the creep, and then he sees with heartbroken familiarity the broken condom and before he

even thinks, he's saying, Lookit, a rubba! and the Big Man
kicks the scrap of latex out into the street, his beautiful
shoe barely missing the face of the man squatting by him,
and the Chilean brings down the Buick, they shove him
around and point to the roof, shove him around some
more, throw a clutch of bills at his green plastic chair,
Chinese-fire-drill themselves into the humped Buick sitting low with cheap-suited muscle, peeling out fast at first,
then slowing, passing, one last look out the car windows at
the rooftops along the street, their eyes looking high above
you, you in your naked insomnia in your dark, wide-flung
french door windows to the apartment you will never in
your life be able to afford, you grab your dick at them, you
give them the finger, you spit at them, and when they are
gone, you sit and wait on the corner of the bed, playing
with the pistol, waiting for the trash truck, the bakery, a
robbery, the dawn.

never in
this world

We were stuck in the sand along a sideroad to a swamp cabin, me and the girl I was trying to get something from, her feet up on the dashboard, a hand of mine up the back of her pretty purple sweater. I had started telling her ghost stories. That usually worked although this was no ordinary girl. She was from out of town. And this is what she said, she said she thought it was a symptom of her own self-absorption that she was unable to see other people's ghosts. She said to tell her a true ghost story, one where even she could have seen the ghost.

I said, Well, you know, not all ghosts are the white vapor kind. I said some are balls of fire that circle the ceilings of a room in an old house and some are just dishrags left at the bottom of the staircase every morning. Every morning so that you know it is not a dog because you have put the dog out, and you know it is not a child because you have no children, and you know it is not mice, and on and on. You know that it is a ghost because it becomes an annoyance, the ache in your back from bending over every morning, the television program you are interrupted from by the form passing the door.

This is where the girl stopped me and my hand again. She asked me what I was leading up to.

I said, Okay, mostly all I have are true stories about dead people I knew well who have something weird or funny lingering in their deaths, okay? I said, The ghost part is up to you to conjure. I said I had a true story about something that happened along the road we were stuck on, did she want to hear it, and she said, Is this a true story or a ghost story, and I said I was pretty sure it was probably both.

All right, let's have it, she said, settling back into the seat. This was no ordinary girl.

A bunch of us were down at the swamp cabin sitting around one night, beer and whiskey, a bowl of reefer on the table, another chair thrown on the fire. It wasn't as

much a party as it was a long brooding kind of night together, one where after a while somebody will just stand up
quickly to stagger and lurch slamming out the door with no
one even looking up from their glasses. That's what our
friend Guy, long blond hair strings, year-round red flannel
shirt, joint-behind-the-ear type of friend Guy did, he just
stood up lurching out the door saying he'd just walk home.
We barely remember him leaving.

The girl said, Scared to death so far.

I said, You should be because he just disappeared.

She stopped me. What do you mean just disappeared,
she said.

I said disappeared in that he hasn't been seen since,
disappeared in that the police were called in and we spent
hours ourselves last fall looking for him. It was foggy and
the police went to the sawmill to ask any log-truck drivers
if they had seen anything, picked up any hitchhikers, anything like that, but they had seen no one, they said, and
they are about the only traffic on these roads late at night,
throttling up from the big woods of Carolina. We walked
the shoulders of the main road looking for any clue that
Guy had taken off through the swamp or fallen in a quicksand ditch. We walked the road shoulders all the way from
the cabin back into town and it is a distance of some miles.

So what about the ghost, said the girl, disengaging us a little with a look out the window.

I guess that's for you and me to conjure, I said. I said I really didn't know how to anticipate Guy's ghost. Guy was too laid-back for apparition. He would have said he wouldn't want to disturb anyone's groove. He was too stoned most of the time for some dishrag gesture of irony. Guy's ghost would have to be what he himself would have wanted it to be, something like a cartoon.

So I'm on the lookout for a cartoon come wafting through the woods, said the girl, folding her pretty purple sweater into a pillow.

I'm not sure, I said, the talk about Guy bringing me down a certain measure.

We said nothing. It was quiet.

So, said the girl, is that the weird true ghost story or was that the funny dead ghost story?

I said, Well, I have sort of a funny dead criminal ghost story. There was this guy I knew, Johnny, who is dead, and his ghost only seems to appear to me. I mean, you could see his ghost but you wouldn't know what it was.

How does this work, said the girl.

It's like I said about not all ghosts being the white vaporous kind, and I'm not sure if Johnny was smart enough for dramatic manifestation. Also, poor Johnny was dyslexic, which gives his ghost its spin.

Try again, the girl said, and I moved to her.

Once Johnny was the first mate on a trawler, I was winchman. I was supposed to be sleeping during his watch but he would sneak down the hatch ladder to my bunk and wake me, have me come up to the wheelhouse. Read the charts for me, he'd say. Read the loran for me. Are we lost?

So I would smoke a few cigarettes from his pack, it was near the end of a long trip and he was selling them for fifty dollars apiece. I would plot the chart, read the loran. On the last day of the trip we were low on fuel heading home. I was dead tired from my watches and sitting up through half of Johnny's, and I wouldn't let him on the last day rouse me from my bunk. Later I came out grumpy on deck to stow gear and break the hatches. Johnny was up on the widowwalk. He flicked a hundred-dollar-now cigarette butt down at me. It was a brilliant day, eighteen hours toward home, until I saw that the sun was shining in the wrong part of the sky. Continents spun around us, we were closer to England than to the inlet of our home.

And someone killed him for that, said the girl.

Almost, I said. I almost did, for one. But I tell you this so that you can understand why we thought it was so funny to us later that anyone could take Johnny seriously enough to have him killed. It was later in the year. Fishing had fallen off. Johnny put a crew together, mostly kids, to take a trawler down to Colombia. It was reefer. They all expected a tropical paradise of green water and clean beaches, and what they found when they finally got there were twelve-foot seas and rain, miles and miles of ragged rocks, a shoreline of mountains. They weren't even sure they had pulled into the right bay marked on some suspect charts. They laid at anchor hungry for two days, and no one came out to meet them. The night before they were going to say Fuck it and steam to Mexico for fuel, a bunch of dugout diesel canoes motored out. These enormous Indians leapt over the railings, and pretty soon more dugout canoes came loaded with bales and bales of pot. My friend said one Indian who they put to work in the hold was so tall that even standing down in the main hatch his head stuck out above the deck, and he could hold whole bales under each arm. The Indians were supposed to give Johnny fuel and fresh food. The last canoe brought a barrel of oil and a string of live chickens.

Johnny barely brought them back. They shook the Coast Guard in a hurricane remnant, but a kid was thrown against a bulkhead and badly broke his arm. They were swindled for fuel in the Bahamas, and somewhere just in the lower curve of the Carolina coast Johnny lost his nerve. He pulled into an inlet, called the criminals he was working for, then called his older brother, Bucky.

I was drinking with Bucky in the Thirsty Camel, Ocean View, when Bucky got the call. Johnny told him that he had called the main criminals and told them where he would leave the trawler. The main criminals had told Johnny that if he did not bring the trawler up the Chesapeake as was planned that Johnny would be very, very dead, very, very shortly. Bucky came back to the table telling us all this. Everyone at the table at the time, at that moment, was a fisherman. I mean, even if you really weren't, like I really wasn't, that is what we were all doing for money. We had all shipped with Johnny, we all had Johnny stories, and even though Bucky seemed concerned for his little brother, he really didn't mind when we all broke out laughing when he told us the mafia was going to put a contract out on Johnny's life. And even after Bucky told us to finish our drinks and that we were going out to get in his car for the drive down the Carolina coast that night, we were still punching each other in the arm, singing like schoolgirls, "Johnny's getting kee-yulled! Johnny's getting kee-yulled!"

We all felt okay going with Bucky on the Johnny rescue. Bucky was that type of trawler captain: *When in doubt, power out.* Bucky was pretty powerful himself, challenging entire tables of charter-boat fishermen to waltz in the parking lot, passing our table on the way out, telling us to choose a dancing partner.

We found Johnny's trawler tied up to a backwater fishhouse packing pier near Wilmington. The ship was a wreck, reeking of shit and vomit and of the broken arm gone gangrenous. The only overriding smell was the evergreen scent of fresh marijuana. After telling us to clear the decks and cast off the lines, Bucky said to me that the whole thing smelled like Christmas-tree time in a nursing home.

Just off Knots Island we picked up Coast Guard chatter on the radio and it was about us. We saw a premature pinprick of blue light, things glowed toward us on the radar. Out to sea we throttled, ripping back canvas and hatches, hauling out bales with buds like pine cones and shoving them over the side. When the Coast Guard pulled alongside later, we were flooding the empty hold with seawater to flush it, nearly sinking us sitting so low in the water.

So the criminals killed Johnny for that, said the girl.

No, I said, Johnny died of a heroin overdose a couple of months later in New Bedford. His ghost? His ghost is me misspelling my own name, the sun shining in the wrong part of the sky.

The sun crossed the pretty purple sweater as we laid across the seat of the car. It was a fall day, the clouds brilliant. I finally got out and tried to rock us out of the sand while the girl gunned the engine back and forth. We were stuck good.

Come on, let's just walk back into town, I said, and the girl said All right. She was no ordinary girl. We were walking along the highway, actually in the highway because it was Sunday and the sawmill was closed, and we were walking along talking not about ghosts anymore and suddenly, there he was.

There was Guy.

He was about twelve feet long and one lane wide, a barely one-dimensional dark and flanneled pattern in the pavement.

I saw no need to summon Guy's ghost for the girl. I slipped an arm around her and steered us past the apparition, past that annoyance in the asphalt that would have broken our afternoon spell together. We walked and I talked, pointing, the white beards of moss in the trees, the alligator logs in the ditchbank, the cypress nostrils of gloom breathing deep in the dark waters. And as I conjured these things up for her I knew that never in this world would she ever know what she was really giving me then, the spirits she was soothing merely by letting me warm myself against her as we walked.

charity

There was no railing on the bridge. Just a timber-high tire guard. The sedan rode the bridge for an instant, then rolled to rest in the mud below. Undiscovered until dawn, the child broken, the woman dead.

The child waited the charity-ward calendar for someone to claim him, his legs in plaster and braced to his neck. Babble and drool and suppers of boiled oats and soft eggs was Cleft Palate Week. Blind Month was like a party game, uncertain hands shaking the child awake as they groped the side rails of his bed trying to find their own. The child waited Splayed Hip Month, Faceless Weekend, the Undescended Testicle Day. Burn Month was in summer. Children tearing a favorite toy apart and thrashing it to the floor, nuns in the midst of the screaming, first with ointment and ice, then syringes. Even injected, the thrashing and the noises, something like flesh on flesh in the beds, bright reds and whites.

The child made friends with a boy with a tail. The boy stole small things from the covers of the coma children for them to play with. The doctors were going to cut off the boy's tail, the boy said, and when he asked, the nuns told him it would be buried in a cemetery by a priest. When the boy asked if he would be permitted to attend the funeral the nuns had said no, that his soul was not in his tail.

Then I am going to run away, confided the boy to the broken child, the tail twitching the pants leg it was tucked into.

When it came time for the boy with the tail they caught him by surprise. The nuns lifted him from his breakfast tray and fastened him into a gown. The broken child waved as they pushed him past on the table with wheels. Later, the boy came back with his tail. What he was missing in his bed were his legs.

You told them! the boy accused the broken child. I am going to kill you, the boy said, his tail still swimming its nervous search of the empty sheets.

I am getting better, the boy with the tail told the

broken child in Recovery Row. You'd better not sleep at night.

At night the child watched the boy with the tail's bed. At the doorway to the ward a nun snored across an open book, a flashlight and a teacup in the blue gloom. The child watched an arm rise up quickly and throw from the covers across the way, and then he would feel the scramble of a roach on his face. Hundreds the size of fingers lived in the bedside urinals. The broken child would try to catch the roach before it crawled down into his plaster and nested. Catch! A quick rise and whisper, Catch! until a sweep of flashlight made them still.

Brain Month the boy with the tail ate from the trays around him. I am getting strong, whispered the boy with the tail. I eat everything to make me strong. You better be strong, he told the broken child. You better say your prayers to meet Jesus. Around them brainless arms waved hello and good-bye.

The holiday Christmas was in Reformatory Month. Hourly bed checks at night and stolen clothing. Fistfights in the showers and worse. A fire in the laundry, a nun nearly blinded with a fork. They all loved the boy's tail. They leaned on his bed rails, farmers along a fence, and felt it.

I paid them money to kill you for me, the boy with the tail told the broken child. They are going to get you at night, you snitch, and strangle you and kill you.

You don't have any money, said the broken child, and the boy with the tail opened a fist and showed him a penny.

The missionaries came at Christmas with oranges and little plastic crosses for the children to play with. They gave the broken child an extra orange because the boy with the tail had told them confidentially that the child was not expected to live long.

The Lord claim and protect your soul, the missionaries said.

α lαdγ came to play a flute and showed the children pictures of animals in a book. Look, there's you, they would scream at a child who had a snout like a pig. Look, there's you, they said to a child who looked like an animal with tusks. Look, there's you, they said to a blind child who said, What, what do I look like?

The lady was closing the book and trying to leave when the boy with the tail said, Look, there's me! What is that thing? and the lady looked in the book and said, That is a picture of a monkey. They can climb and hang by their tail. Yes, that's me, that's me, said the boy with the tail.

You weren't even in the book, the boy said to the broken child as the woman fled.

Feed me bananas and peanuts, the boy with the tail told the nuns. I am a monkey. I can hang by my tail. Look at what I can do. The boy went from bed rail to bed rail with his tail. Soon I will learn how to hang from lights and spin from the fan. One night you'll wake up and see me hanging above your bed, he told the broken child. It will be too late for you then. Out the door I'll run away through the trees. No one will ever catch me and nobody will ever care about you.

The broken child begged the nuns to find his mother. She's with Jesus, they kept telling him. The nuns had called the army and found a father for the child. The father raked parade-ground pebbles all day, his mind dimmed by artillery. Call someplace else, the army had told the nuns and had hung up the call.

One night there was noise. The boy with the tail was on the floor. He fell out of bed, the nun told the broken child.

charity

I was coming for you, said the boy with the tail to the child.

When they cut the child out of his plaster it was Extra Limb Month. There were visitors. When they cut the broken child out of his plaster they discovered that his legs had become stiff sticks of long black hair. Interesting, said the visitors before they looked at the boy with the tail.

They made a little cart on casters so the broken child could push himself along in the halls and wait. He would roll to the top of the long hall to charity ward. When he would see the truck with the trays of food coming he would roll down the hall singing, Tray Truck! Tray Truck! He was no longer frightened of the boy with the tail. The boy with the tail had left with the visitors. With the money the visitors gave to the nuns, the nuns bought a grandfather clock. It stands alone in the long hallway down to charity ward. To this day it keeps perfect time.

plymouth rock

I have seen the future of law enforcement in
this country and it is my brother Douglas.
Douglas, wired in, sound through his ear, mi-
crophone in his lapel, those reflective fixed-
stare glasses. Pushes through crowds clearing
path, flashing heat, fanning open his oversize
Sears sport coat to see this machine pistol
strapped to his side like life support. Flashing
the heat, flashing the heat, fanning a few fears
of death by dumdum bullet.

Everybody is so proud of Douglas. Douglas doesn't speak to me. I have not even seen
Douglas until today. I am down to the store
for a six-pack and a magazine. Out of nowhere
Douglas and this gorilla push me up against
plate glass. Douglas says, Listen you creep, we

got our eye on you. Douglas says, We got people watching you to take you out. Douglas says when the president comes through our town I'd better stay the hell at home. Douglas says, Don't walk the streets, don't snap your gum, don't even fart in the president's general direction. Then Douglas slaps the sunglasses off my face. See, he says to the gorilla, he's got assassin eyes, all right.

Douglas drops me on the sidewalk, they drive away in one of those plain-wrapper cars.

Assassin eyes my ass! I say up the street. Everybody says I have my mother's eyes. I take after my mother's side of the family. Her brothers, my uncles, like to drink and party and mess up their lives as much as I do. Douglas takes after Dad.

Like last Thanksgiving, when I saw Douglas last, I was lounging around in my George Jetson bathrobe having a few bloodies watching the parade on TV. Douglas comes in making a big deal of taking off his coat to flash me some heat. He's got on underneath a Teflon plastic-laminated armor vest. I said, Douglas, man, why don't you take a drink with me and chill? Douglas doesn't drink. They give him piss tests all the time for everything. I say, Douglas, come on in here and watch the parade. You'd like this,

Douglas, they got the superhero balloons coming down Fifth Avenue. They got Underdog and everything.

I go on like this until it is time to eat. Mother says it's okay for me to wear George Jetson to the table as long as my hair is combed.

Dad carves the bird, I'm into the Sauterne. Mother asks someone to say grace. I look at Douglas. I am thinking, I am wondering, What is it in someone's past that snaps their mind into law enforcement? I wonder was it me? Mother and Dad always punishing Douglas for not keeping his little brother out of trouble, not stopping me putting out Bobby Van's eye with the BB, not stopping me and Buddy Burnette throwing that costume dummy in front of cars Halloween. Then, when we were good, just sitting around the dirt pile, Douglas would come out of the house to neutralize us, put me and Buddy Burnette in choke holds, practice some of that comic-book mail-order jujitsu until one of us would puke.

Douglas and I grew up so different. Douglas was into airplanes he hung from the ceiling on thread. These big black Nazi bombers, the folded-wing fighters, little fire in the guns and bombs that dropped.

One time Mother's brother Uncle Kip came over for

the Cutchins' patio party next door. Uncle Kip got so loaded they had to put him in my room and I slept in Douglas's room. Laid in Douglas's bed, Douglas's thread-borne Luftwaffe lit like over London by the Cutchins' patio light next door. I snoozed for a while and when I woke up the party was out, everyone had gone home. I laid there and looked up, these big black things were doing slow turns on the breeze, just hanging there, waiting to feed off your face if you fell back asleep. Last Thanksgiving I was re-membering. I looked at Douglas wondering, What a way for a kid to have himself go to sleep every night, and Doug-las just looked back with a look to flash me some heat.

Me, I was a ship man myself. In my room I built the *Cutty Sark* and *Kearsarge*, the *Royal Hind* and the *Yankee Clipper*, these big Japanese battleships from Japan. I never had any floating around on display. Buddy Burnette and I always burned them up in dirt-pile sea battles. There is this rocking chair in the corner of my room Mother used to rock me in when I was a child. I would kind of kneel in it backwards and grab the two wooden knobs like they were a ship's wheel. I would rock back and forth in heavy seas, leaning over when the ship lunged into the waves. I would rock back and forth and make wind noise and water sounds like hissing foam. The waves would crash the bow and try to wash me away overboard. People would yell, Help, help, like my mate, then they would all get washed away, and I would almost go over myself as I rocked back and forth and braced for another wave, until one time in the middle of a hurricane I was swept into the sea on the floor. Mother came upstairs to see what all the Help-yelling and wave-and-wind noise were about. She saw me swimming across the floor. I was only foaming at the mouth for effect. That one shipwreck capped off all she needed to know to send me to see Dr. Harriet Frech, kiddie psychiatrist.

I won't say it was all just that. There were some other conditions. There was a condition with Douglas. There were some teachers at school. Miss Mauk. Miss Mauk said for us to do the Pilgrims coming to Plymouth Rock. I was in my Oriental ocean phase from some *National Geographics* Uncle Kip had brought over for me. I painted the Pilgrims pulling up to the New World in Chinese junks complete with retread tires lashed to their sides, their black-and-white laundry starched in the rigging. The Pilgrims were tying up to a dock that the Indians were running with gas pumps and signs that said LIVE BAIT and COLD BEER. Miss Mauk sent the picture home to the folks with a note that said maybe they ought to have me looked at. Dr. Frech gave me all these secret test patterns. They let me back into school on the condition Douglas would keep an eye on his little brother.

I was thinking about all this last Thanksgiving when Mother was asking around for somebody to say grace. I was looking at Douglas. Douglas was looking back. I said, Mother, Douglas is flashing me heat at the table again, and Mother said, Douglas, please, and Douglas said, Aw, he's just a drunk you should have thrown out of the house long ago.

I stood up. I stretched my George Jetson arm over to Douglas across the table. Go ahead and break it, I said. I know it will make you feel better.

My arm and Douglas go back to high school. Nobody really liked Douglas then. Whistle while you work, Douglas is a jerk-type of thing walking down the halls. Douglas wanted to run for sergeant-at-arms for student assembly. Don't do it, I begged him. People will really think you are an asshole. I tried to help him. Me and Buddy Burnette tore down all his campaign posters, but he won anyway, running unopposed. At the first student assembly they tried to reorganize the student government. There were lots of motions and amendments just to stay out of class. Douglas stood in the back of the auditorium waiting for a signal from our principal, Lewis K. Smith, to eject somebody out.

Lewis K. Smith kept having to stand up and say, If there is no order soon, everybody is going back to homeroom. Finally I raised my hand and even though it was me, they had to call on me because they were being so strict on rules of order.

I stood up from where I was sitting with Buddy Burnette and I said to settle the student crisis I proposed to abolish the entire government and install Lewis K. Smith as King of the School. Buddy Burnette stood up and shouted, The king is dead! Long live King Smith! because we had been studying France. The phys-ed coach and Douglas came down the aisle to eject us out, except that in his eagerness, Douglas did something comic book to my arm that snapped it in two places and I had to go to the hospital.

So last Thanksgiving I offered across the table to Douglas my arm to break as a sort of peace offering. Everybody said for me to sit down, say grace, eat my turkey.

everybody was so excited the day the gorillas came to town to interview about Douglas being able to flash some heat. They interviewed Lewis K. Smith, Miss Mauk, the

Cutchins. Then they were coming over to interview the family. I was upstairs in my George Jetson, combing my hair. I had my file on Douglas in a Blue Horse notebook. I had the Nazi bomber decals, the jujitsu mail-order clippings, an eighth-grade picture of Buddy Burnette. I waited for them to call me downstairs with my Douglas file. I happened to look out the window and the gorillas were backing out of our drive. I ran downstairs spilling open my Blue Horse notebook, my carefully detailed sketching of the dirt-pile neutralizations everywhere.

I was thinking about all this last Thanksgiving, Mother and Dad asking Douglas over dinner what the president was really like. Tell us one thing, one little thing, they said. Douglas looked at me and wiped his mouth and said, I really shouldn't be telling anyone this. I drained my wine glass. Douglas said they had code names for everybody. He said, You'd never guess what the code name is for the president. I looked at Mother and Dad and beheld their complete cluelessness.

Douglas said, We call the president Red Rider. Mother says What? Dad said, Douglas says they call the president the Red Rider. Mother says, Red Rider? Isn't that what the boys used to play in the front yard? Red Rider? Didn't Douglas give Buddy Burnette a concussion playing Red

Rider? Dad said, No it was Red Rover the boys used to play. Dad says it was me who Douglas gave the concussion to. Douglas says It's just a code, Red Rider, that's all it is, just a code. Mother wants to know did Buddy Burnette's parents make us pay for sending Buddy to the hospital playing Red Rider. She says it would have been just like them to. Dad says it was Red Rover, Red Rover. Like Red Rover, Red Rover, send somebody over. Douglas said, Red Rider, it's just a code, just a code they used.

I stood up. I had forgotten to put the concussion in my Blue Horse book. I stepped on the dog, tripped over the cat, stomped the stairs to my room. I kneeled in my chair and I prayed.

Help me with my future, Lord. Help me with my grassy knolls.

Help me with the sounds like paper sacks popping.

Brighten my brother's eyes to seek mine out in the curbside crowds.

Flash me some heat, Lord, for I have seen my future, and it is my brother Douglas.

tunga tuggo, lingua dingua

When Cyphus looked up from his raking and saw the black park ranger with his Smokey the Bear hat and his park service flashlight hip-mounted, a little cockily, like a faux-fire-arm, in his heart of hearts Cyphus thought, This will either be Attitude or Uncle Tom. He said to young Samuel, Just let me do the talking. Samuel said weren't they lucky they had not bought the shovel, just the rakes, and Cyphus said it had not been *luck* that they had not bought the shovel, that he had *had* the sixteen dollars for the shovel, that it was just Samuel's *deficit of information* concerning the location of their mutual father, more importantly, their mutual father's *wallet* buried somewhere in these dunes. Cyphus asked, said furthermore, had Samuel ever *shoveled* sand before? and Samuel had said not really, and Cyphus explained, Sand just keeps filling itself in when you dig it, and when it's wet, forget it. Besides, having the rakes on the park preserve was bad enough, just let him do the talking.

Hello! Cyphus called out in an ignorant touristy welcome-wagon sort of way, aware suddenly of the street clothes he was wearing, and young Samuel's cheap Mexican sombrero, way out in the preserve where no one ever came. They had walked long, and for Samuel, painful, sandy miles leaving their car, their father's old limousine, at the end of the asphalt. The park ranger said, Ya'll not digging up sea oats, are you? and Cyphus said no, no, they had seen the signs along the first quarter mile of trail, signs that said SEA OATS ARE PROTECTED, NO FIRES, NO TRESPASSING AFTER DARK, WILD PONIES KICK AND BITE. The park ranger looked at Cyphus, looked at bashful sombrero-headed Samuel with his red rake and cumbersome-shod clubfoot, and then looked out over the autumn ocean. The ocean was as black and white as far and as boring as you could see.

No, no sea oats, Officer, Cyphus said finally, bouncing his rake a little in the tideline on its SuperResilient tines. Cyphus wiped at nothing in his eye so he could read WEST-

BROOK on the park ranger's breastplate, but thought it a little early to use this information to work the ranger yet, so he tried this: Cyphus said, Are you from Baltimore? because Cyphus prided himself on his ear for accents, his ability to discern Emporia from west Tidewater where the peanuts give way to tobacco, and the park ranger said Philadelphia, and Cyphus nodded his head knowingly in his knowing-dumbhead-nod. But my *mother's* from Baltimore, the park ranger said, so Cyphus brightened and bravely bent his SuperResilient tines into the sand, leaning farmer-like on the handle end and said, So, you can say *Baltimorean* was spoken in the home? The ranger looked at Cyphus and said, Don't y'all be digging up the sea oats, and he nimbly long-stepped up the steep face of the nearest dune in a way that would leave most people breathless from the effort, most people slogging up, grasping and ripping out sea oats to pull themselves along. Cyphus knew the ranger would linger just over the duneline, and the ranger knew Cyphus knew, and to establish this known fact Cyphus hollered over the duneline, So how many acres *are* in the preserve? and the ranger's disembodied head appeared Smokey Bear-hatted and it looked out over Cyphus and Samuel into the black-and-whiteness, calculating, the head saying it expected it to be about twenty-two thousand acres, and Cyphus said, And how much of that is in sand? and the head said, Most all of it, and from his vowel rhythm Cyphus figured his father from south Jersey, maybe. The ranger held a wave, a hand that stayed on the duneline for a couple of moments after the head had disappeared, and Cyphus called out, Thank you, Officer Westbrook!

Twenty-two *thousand* acres, and you wanted to buy a shovel, Cyphus said to Samuel, Samuel who called himself a rocket scientist, living with an older sister in nearly condemned government housing outside the Redstone arsenal, Samuel able to give a patient listener the step-by-step evolution of the Apollo moon program beginning with the friendly internment of the V-2 Germans down in Huntsville after the war, a little of Samuel's lineage vapor-trailing around there, Samuel denying this heritage anytime Cyphus professed an interest in hearing the genuine accent of a rocket Nazi crossed with an Alabama manure spreader.

Let's just go home, Samuel said, saying *home* when he was tired instead of *hideout* when he was not, the place where they slept in fact being neither, just a family beach house where no one really knew where they were and didn't really care, no one except the jury of relatives waiting at the family beach house every day for some report on the missing father, and more importantly, some pieces of paper gone missing with the missing father's wallet. These were relatives from three bloodlines, heirs of clouded sorts, eating and waiting, crab eggs, bacon dumplings, fried gourd, they would announce—chowchow, satsuma jack, beezle sticks, fixings from another planet, Cyphus would think as the platters were passed around in the morning, adding, saying to himself, arrhythmic heart, gouted foot, bloody stool. And in the evening, Cyphus and Samuel would "hide" the old limousine among some dumpsters, except on Thursdays, walk up the beach path just past sunset, and there they all would be, already out watching the rock-salt moon they had hung in the sky that week, lined up in those new high-back console plastic porch chairs they all hated, their white hair like helmets, globes of blue filaments lit by a single streetlight flickering on, one or two teased-up heads especially halo-like, glowing and ready for departure. Hello! Cyphus would always call out in an attempt to mask his empty-handedness, and always everyone could hear nearly deaf Aunt Marty hiss, Shit.

Well, we not *going* home, Cyphus said, Cyphus dropping the contracted "are" in unconscious deference to Officer Westbrook, We not going home mainly because I can't stand the way they all talk anymore, those south-harbor phonics and peanut-roll drawl, god, the drool on Uncle Reston's bib, too, god.

I don't mind talking to them, said Samuel, him the only of the pair the relatives spoke to, them speaking to him of the beach-house improvements, the washer-dryer the spouses of the incontinent all chipped in for, the electronic atmospheric-weather wind-and-rain station on the roof. Yes, where *is* that old junky thing on the wall Dad used to tap in the mornings, always wrong forecast, them eager enough to chuck his vestiges out as soon as he disappeared, thought Cyphus shouldering his rake, leading the march carward. Chuck his vestiges *out!* "*Out*" having two and a half syllables with a prominent "a" vowel sound best achieved when one's jaws are set in a static howling embouchure, them claiming their aches and pains better barometers than the spring-loaded kind anyway, which reminded them, when Cyphus asked, where the old junky thing was, of the time when they had to wrap Aunt Irma in a rubber sheet when she died, was that scarlet fever or smallpox? The virus alive for sixteen years in some old books they forgot to burn, and Cousin Gernice, greedy Cousin Gernice, took the books she wasn't 'sposed to, and her child now dead from page-thumbing (or most likely cover-chewing, or *worse* if it was a Gernice child), that'll teach you, Cyphus, about greed and reading too, so that Cyphus had to leave the porch quickly, rubbing the soft spot on his head, heading out to the beach where young Samuel flipped jellyfish over in the surf wash with his horned, callused clubfoot, ghosty things in the dim reaches of the streetlight, Samuel saying the top of the jellies were harmless, that it was only the tentacled bottom side that would scald your skin with neurotoxin, Samuel flipping one over and picking it up, holding it like a pie he was about to slap into Cyphus's face. Drop that jelly, had said Cyphus, put it down, I want to talk to you, and You too, said Samuel. Samuel said he had caught the drift it was believed their father was buried somewhere in the preserve dunes with his wallet and pieces of family paper and Cyphus said he had not heard that, but he *did* have the feeling that none of the pieces of family paper had his or Samuel's names on them, Cyphus beginning to explain his waning enthusiasm, beginning to resent their mantle of step-and-fetch-itism, Cyphus and Samuel the centrifugally thrown family outcasts from this tidewater outpost of thirteenth-son Anglospawn, Samuel in Alabama and Cyphus *up Nawth*, come down to pick through the leavings and cold trails and postulations from them who porch-sit and

talk about everything but It, the Thang of the missing father, the disappearance and supposed death, six days in the
newspaper and no leads, and most tragically, no long black
wallet well-oiled with greasy fingers spreading it open to
purchase shit-property below list price from coloreds, for
coloreds (by coloreds? them that knew Father put in the
air, look at the nostril-flare and lip-fat on that son), just get
the wallet so they could all go home. Like the lady who
came to claim her drowned husband in the freak charter-
boat rollover just offshore, twenty-five folk tipped off the
upended decks into the sea, almost all drowning drunk,
and more than one wife coming down to the harbor police
office where the dead fishermen were laid out on the ferry
benches, coming down just to fetch the car keys and the
money-stuffed wallets out of the drowned sportfishermen's
pockets, the one saying over her shoulder, leaving, to the
harbor police sergeant when he asked about the disposition
of the body, her saying, He like fish so much, feed him to
them. That's us, you and me, Samuel, Cyphus said, fish
wives come to fetch, and to tell you the truth, I'm getting
tired of it, tired of the way people talk to us, saying, Just die
off, you and your family. Just be dead, is what people told
Cyphus and Samuel as they poked around and made their
inquiries, someone obviously having to spell it out to their

father so he would understand it well enough; the father's ransacked house, his gutted office, him gone missing, some people even saying the previous weekend at a fish fry that Cyphus and Samuel had reconnoitered that of all the people born in the area, no one since Nat Turner had needed killing as much, further stating that it was unfortunate the body (the word "body" implying to Cyphus's junior-detective mind father-flesh-corruption rather than hightail-antic), unfortunate that the body had not yet been found so that they could saw off the head with a jagged cypress board and pike it on some crossroads somewhere, maybe near the new Wal-Mart, icon against housing shod artists, hog-farmer shysters intent on letting negroes have a place to live with paved roads and fire hydrants, goddamn it, and looking closer, leaning in, spilling their draft beer out of their paper cups onto Samuel's and Cyphus's shoes, on closer inspection, didn't Samuel look a *lot* like their father, and suddenly Cyphus saw how it could all turn ugly, pitchforks and cattail torches, hunting them down through the swamp with baying hounds and bad postures, to hack off Samuel's head in absentia, a passable reproduction, a Pappy likeness, the hacking off achieving the desired aging process to bring the item current, so they fled the fish fry, kept to the anonymous interstates and off the secondary roads at night, hiding the limousine amongst the dumpsters in the evenings except on Thursdays, going home to the beach cottage they were beginning to call their hideout, to their own people, the sort willing to wrap their own kind in rubber sheets and burn them as a matter of convenience like household rubbish out back of the family place, a place where Cyphus told Samuel they were absolutely not going back to that night and maybe never again. Period.

So Cyphus and Samuel began walking back to their father's limousine, stopping every once in a while to rake at a driftwood hand, or cowrie shell ear, or a spinal column of old rope, the whole time Cyphus feeling Officer Westbrook's spying eyes just over the wind-sharpened dune line. Cyphus felt suddenly unlucky, that Officer Westbrook may have recognized them as Darrell Dontell Boyd progeny, Samuel's thumb-spread putty cheeks, his own slouch beneath chip-bearing shoulders, something in the way Officer Westbrook looked into their faces and then fixed on a point in the black-and-white ocean, a pixel dot in a missing-persons newspaper-photo-composite shot they were congenitally part of. Damn, Smokey Bear hat here, Smokey Bear hat there, how did he move back and forth so quickly on either side of the trail when the trail turned inland, the mystery revealed when Cyphus heard a horse bluster, or whatever he thought that blowout snort noise they make is called. They were tired and the sun was filing itself off on the rough smog edge of the horizon. Cyphus was ready for a drink, Samuel's painful clubfoot had him nearly teary-eyed. They arrived through the last sand walkway to the park preserve parking lot and immediately saw that someone had stolen their car.

cyphus was anticipating a couple of paperwork problems at the ranger station. Cyphus himself would not have reported the car stolen if not so pressed by Officer Westbrook after Officer Westbrook watched Cyphus and Samuel walk around bewildered looking into the sand where the car had been as if the earth had opened and somehow swallowed it there. If it had been just Cyphus, alone, he would have hiked on out to the highway where he had seen a little roadhouse tavern and called a cab or hitched a ride to the Greyhound station and made his way back to New York. He had been for quitting this quest altogether, you remember. But there had been Officer Westbrook with his little Chincoteague pony and there had been Samuel with his clubfoot and there had been the car stolen off federal property, and soon they were trundling through the sand to Officer Westbrook's ranger station, darkness on them. Samuel's clubfoot had him almost openly weeping so Officer Westbrook let him ride the pony but the large red plastic rakes spooked the horse. It would not budge unless Cyphus walked in front of him, so Cyphus led the way, the rakes fanned out in front of him, Officer Westbrook leading the bridled pony, Samuel beatifically atop, Cyphus looking back occasionally and thinking it was all a little too damn much like Joseph and Mary and Palm Sunday all rolled up together for his taste.

The paperwork problems Cyphus was anticipating were going to arise from two things: Cyphus had no registration because he supposed the registration was still with his father in the long black wallet, or in the glove compartment, or in the possession of his father's longtime driver, Mr. Buck; and secondly, probably more problematic, Cyphus and Samuel had driven the car off a federal impound lot in Portcity after it had been seized by federal agents following Darrell Dontell Boyd's disappearance. Cyphus and Samuel had gone there just to look in the trunk for the wallet with the pieces of family paper in it, and the keys were tucked in the visor and the chain-link gate was open. Cyphus jumped in, commanded the hesitant Samuel to do the same, and they drove off the lot. No one tried to stop them because no one was around. Things like that happen. It was lunchtime.

The Boyd relatives had been much encouraged, at first, when Cyphus and Samuel pulled up to the beach cottage in the old limousine. The last it had been heard of was from Mr. Buck's incoherent recollections of where he had left it before being roughed up by the Navy SEALS, Mr. Buck's story of Darrell Dontell Boyd's last sighting evolving constantly but not entirely suspiciously yet because everyone knew all about Mr. Buck, eighty-eight years old and never sober past age fourteen. Mr. Buck drove our city's boulevards diverting traffic into medians and people's yards as he scrunched his neck, rolling eyeballs skyward to watch for explosive fuel tanks falling off Navy trainers, having had a close call once, certain his fate would be a fiery one, his clothes sprayed with flame retardant so that in the hot weather he smelled like a kerosene leak in a homeless shelter. Mr. Buck lived in the limousine, slept in the back waiting for Dontell Boyd, bathed occasionally in Dontell Boyd's garage whenever Dontell insisted, Mr. Buck's few possessions, some canned goods, a canteen, paperbacks, pint-bottle stash, were kept in a Derby Farms tomato box in the trunk. Mr. Buck ate his cheese-cracker breakfasts during his daily morning cry squatting head bent against the front bumper. In this way, the Boyd relatives long considered Mr. Buck an unashamed moocher.

Officer Westbrook's office was a brown-painted plywood parks department toolshed add-on with sun-damaged windows and little cheap trifold brochures depicting the abundant vermin-like wildlife. Cyphus relaxed. No computer, no telephone, no one else there but the three of them past closing time to fill out the federal form for Lost Property, that form being one of the three Officer Westbrook had in his five-generation government desk with the sticking drawers, the second form to be signed by hikers agreeing not to hold the federal government liable if on the seventeen-mile nature hike through razor scrub and quicksand one would be gored by wild tusked boar, succumb to heat maladies, be struck by lightning, or be bitten by one or more of the four poisonous snakes indigenous to and plentiful in the park preserve. The third form in Officer Westbrook's desk was an application for summer employment.

What galled Cyphus as he filled in the fictions of his life on the Lost Property form was the developing friendliness between Officer Westbrook and Samuel. They had been talking all along the trail and now Cyphus noticed they came courting toward one another across the South by stretching their regional tongues, so to speak, so they would touch, so to speak. Samuel was straining his long *o*'s to roll them up from Huntsville across Asheville and Officer Westbrook had dropped the *i-n-g* ring down from Baltimore through Richmond hooking a right at Charlotte to meet Samuel somewhere around Hickory, North Carolina. Somehow they had run an old wives' tale about caterpillar hair as a cold-weather indicator into a crawling sexual metaphor and were laughing a little too damn freely for Cyphus's taste as he tried to make up an insurance serial number and scratch it from the end of a faulty Darrell Dontell Boyd–for–Assembly TIME TO BOIL OFF SOME OF THE FAT ink pen he had found in the front seat of the limousine. He could not wait to get Samuel outside and pinch his arm.

Why don't you and Officer Westbrook just get a room together? Cyphus said to young Samuel as they waited for Officer Westbrook to put up his pony and take them into town. Samuel said Cyphus ought to hear what he sounded like, and Cyphus said he knew what he sounded like because he had recorded himself many times on a reel of tape and Samuel said, You sound homoneurotic, is what you sound like. Samuel told Cyphus he could be nicer to

Officer Westbrook since he was going to take them where they needed to go, and besides, Officer Westbrook had problems at home. First off, said Cyphus, it's the damned least Officer Westbrook can do to give them a ride considering he should spend more time protecting people's cars than snooping over sand dunes making sure they didn't dig up any goddamn sea-oat weeds, and secondly, what kind of problems could Officer Westbrook possibly have at home that would concern Samuel and Samuel said, Shh, here he comes, he got his girlfriend pregnant the very first time they had sex, she was a virgin and it was on a church weekend social.

This is exactly the kind of compassionate quasi-negroidal crap that got our father into the gritty fix he's in somewhere in these dunes, said Cyphus.

Maybe so, said Samuel, but he's going to take us to see Father.

Officer Westbrook's headlights swept out over the low-budget horrorscape in his brand-new four-wheel-drive jeep, Samuel in the front seat jibbering Affirmative Faith nonsense with the park ranger, a doubting Cyphus seething in the backseat, cross-armed, suspecting some sort of homeless Dontell Boyd–lookalike bait-and-switch con game ahead, or at the very least, Officer Westbrook's interest in

Samuel did not range beyond some sort of orthopedophilic predilection. Cyphus was so angry he didn't even kick the sand off his shoes getting into Officer Westbrook's jeep. Where the sandy asphalt deadended into the county highway Cyphus looked up out of his funk at the lights of the little roadhouse tavern and shouted, pointing past the startled heads of Officer Westbrook and Samuel, Wait! Look! There's the car!

Under a penitentiary-strength vapor light beside the Baja Bar, the limousine was parked, or at least, considering its angle of approach, perhaps abandoned. The Baja Bar was a plank-porched place grown out of a chicken-coop watering hole for the local swineherders, the hog muck from their wallow boots scraped off in huge confections on the edges of the front steps. Inside Cyphus would find framed on the walls the original rabid crayonesque constituent letters Baja patrons had sent to editors and legislators concerning all perils, mostly imagined, never thought-out, threatening every arcane aspect of the dynamic hog-farming industry, particularly the growing reluctance on the government's behalf to subsidize sow bellies; there were hog cartoons, hog photographs—hogs in hats, hogs behind the wheel, Miss Pork Products Queen (no Miss Piggy, Cyphus noticed)—all this framed in cheap brass frames adorned with huge screws, all this hanging beneath the cheap nautical crap with that copper cast to it, a couple of ship models frosted with dust and spider-mite-configuration rigging, all of this lending the Baja, Cyphus decided, an "esprit" of pigs at sea.

Cyphus would discover this alone, as Officer Westbrook and Samuel would not get out of the jeep and come into the Baja Bar. The white people who came down to the preserve and asked Officer Westbrook's help and asked him questions were different animals from the ones who collected here at the Baja, the ones collecting here still living "deep country," tall trees hung with long ropes and chains in their lower acres (shade-tree mechanic, they would say), huge cast-iron kettles for boiling down two-hundred-pound-plus fleshly animals (soap making, they would say), scythes, picks, axes handy (because there's always something needing killing on a farm, they would say). Officer Westbrook would wait for Cyphus for a few minutes but he would not go in, and Samuel would not go in, and in this bird-in-the-hand equation, Cyphus decided to cut his losses in favor of retrieving the limousine to drive back up north. Well, then, goodbye, said Samuel, and God bless, said Officer Westbrook.

And good riddance, Cyphus had said, slamming the

jeep door, relieved at relinquishing his role in the wild chasing of Father Goose, already considering how best to hold his red plastic rake so as not to draw attention to it as he entered the bar but also to maintain the rake in some posture of readiness to deploy against the car thief or thieves in case things took their typical ugly turn. He decided nonchalant defiance was the best course. He entered the Baja Bar with the rake shouldered, whistling.

There was only the bartender talking to a waiter at the end of a bar, behind them a huge aquarium filled with silvery moons of a small school of feline-toothed piranha slicing hungrily in one body back and forth across the front glass. No one sat at the booths, and one stool stood pulled away from a wet place on the bar, the wet place floating drinking debris; an empty beer glass, crumpled cigarette pack, ashtray, paperback, and the limousine key ring. The bartender and the waiter stopped talking to stare at Cyphus. There was no music, no sound except the aquarium, air bubbling from a little plastic sea-chest in the coarse sand next to a class ring dropped in for a joke or possibly the result of some macho tequila piranha finger-dipping challenge. The only sound beyond that was a toilet flushing in the rear, then the banging open of the ladies' room door announcing the stumbling exit of a zipper-stuck and muttering Mr. Buck.

Hello! Cyphus offered, entering the place, raised hand, red rake snagging a diving helmet hung from the ceiling like a submarine severed head. Cyphus continued halfway down the bar and sat next to the pulled-out stool, staring at the puddle of beer on the bar soaking the crumpled cigarette pack and the key ring to the limousine. He settled the rake tine-scraping against the foot-rail and waited for Mr. Buck to pinball his way against every six-by-six post that held up the Baja's sheet-metal roof.

Whut's yer poizzin? the bartender spun a cocktail napkin deftly floating in front of Cyphus, Cyphus still watching the sometimes redundant staggering of Mr. Buck ever closer to his bar stool.

I'll have whatever this gentleman is having, Cyphus said.

Hey! shouted the bartender to the waiter. 'E wants whut ta "gintilmun's" habbing!

Gib it to 'um! said the waiter, his tongue licking through a black gap in his gumline.

One *special* comin' yer way! the bartender shouted at Cyphus and Cyphus reached around with his foot for the rake handle, thinking things were off on an ugly dangerous footing here, his accent-spotting needle warped like a compass over iron agate slabbing, the bartender shouting to Mr. Buck, Hey! *Gintilmun*, ya wunt another fuckin' *special*? Mr. Buck frightened himself by withdrawing his hand from his filthy flame-retardant raincoat and mistook his fingers trembling up at his face as dancing serpents. The vision set him in reverse on his journey to the bar stool, all the way back beneath the poster of a Peterbilt blonde in bikini top and jeans cutoffs onto which someone had drawn a crude and uncircumcised penis.

Two specials, comin' right up! shouted the bartender.

Cyphus saw, on a plate by the register with a paper napkin thrown over it, a little plasticine baggie and a short fruit knife, hog tranquilizer cut with strychnine, probably.

Two specials, the bartender said, reminding himself. He bent into the cooler and the piranhas in the aquarium on top of the cooler fluttered themselves against the glass trying to bite off his head. He withdrew a large bag of goldfish and trapped a couple against the side of the clear plastic with a cocktail stirrer. Carefully, he dropped one of the fish into a glass of beer.

One, he said.

Make it a double, said the rotten waiter.

Nue, sir, said the bartender, the *gintilmun* only reques-
tud a special, not a double special. The other fish dripped
onto the floor. The bartender's tremors were making it a
little difficult to trap another fish against the side of the
bag. Commere ya little fuckers, he said, smearing a little
gold into a crease of plastic with the long metal spoon.

Cyphus triangulated the low country swine talk, in-
bred lost-colony white trash mixed with the deserters from
Cornwallis's prison army at Yorktown, getting a fix on the
bartender, the rotten tooth waiter having maybe one par-
ent of certified tobacco road trailer trash. Cyphus was of a
mind to ease nearer the limousine keys when he felt a
skeletal hand grab his shoulder, pulling a clutch of his
shirt.

Hello! said Cyphus to Mr. Buck when Mr. Buck was
mostly on the stool next to him and able to release
Cyphus's shirt that he seemed to have forgotten he was
holding on to. Cyphus's greeting bolted Mr. Buck upright
and awake, and in deference to using Cyphus's shoulder to
leverage himself up to the bar, he scowled at Cyphus with a
long moment of exaggerated recognition he was completely unable to disguise.

Don't you dare touch me, hissed Mr. Buck, leaning
independently now on his filthy, chemical-smelling rain-

coat elbows, trying to cut what he thought were menacing eyes toward the weak-smiling Cyphus.

Laying a hand on me would be mistake number one for you, he said. *Where's my drink?* he suddenly shouted, mostly into Cyphus's face.

Her' we go, two specials, and the bartender set the foamy glasses down with hands that rocked the swimming fish inside like tidal currents. Cyphus raised his finger to point at the goldfish pecking the bottom of the lagerhead in Mr. Buck's glass but Mr. Buck slapped the hand away.

When people lay a hand on me, like on my shoulder, that's when they're most vulnerable, said Mr. Buck, slowly lifting his dripping glass from the bar top. That's when I grab holt of them and break their fucking wrists.

Mr. Buck's blind mouth sucked in all of the foam and half the beer, including a frantic, backwards-swimming goldfish. He swallowed. Snap, and then snap, he said, licking his lips, and then both your wrists is fucking broke.

Cyphus watched the partially crushed goldfish in his glass weakly drag its entrails through his beer, the little mouth pulsing a slow gaping mute.

Go ahead, said Mr. Buck to Cyphus. The waiter and the bartender watched from the end of the bar. No one was smiling now. Go ahead, just pretend, said Mr. Buck. I won't really break your wrists. Go *on*, gottdamnit, said Mr. Buck and he shoved Cyphus almost off his stool.

Trouble down there, *gintilmun*?

I want another drink, said Mr. Buck, pushing his empty glass toward the bartender.

All we gots tunight's ur specials, said the bartender directly to Cyphus.

Then give me another special, said Mr. Buck.

You got money to pay fur them specials?

Mr. Buck slid into a stance, his hand grinding into the pocket of his human-grease-soaked coarse khakis. First they grab my shoulder, then they grab my arm, that's when I break their wrists, he said. Mr. Buck triumphantly pulled a wad of singles out of his pocket and said to the dollars tenderly, Then I break their knees. He stuffed the money back into his pocket and climbed onto the bar stool. He turned right around to Cyphus.

Sometimes when they're down, I like to kick them in the face, he said.

Charming, said Cyphus.

You going to drink that? Mr. Buck said to Cyphus's dying beer.

Cyphus slid his glass over to Mr. Buck.

I want to ask you about your car, the car out front, said Cyphus.

It ain't for sale, Mr. Buck said.

I know, said Cyphus, it belongs to my father. Have you seen him?

Mr. Buck drained the glass and slammed it down on the bar top. Now I got to piss again, gottdamnit, he announced, and it was clearly Cyphus's fault.

The bartender set two new foaming, swimming specials on the bar in front of Cyphus. Ur what's looking fur yur ol' man?

I was, said Cyphus, and Cyphus found himself drawing one of the glasses toward him in a gesture to inspire camaraderie with this hog farmering-Hessian-descended sadist.

I hurt 'bout sum dawgs diggin' up a bum o'er to the game *pree*serve. Sum ladee touris' spot a thum' stickin' up fum a dune, by the time she got the nigra park ranger ut there the wil' dawgs dun carrit most o' the gud stuff away!

Haw! said the waiter, slapping his hand on the bar.

I'm speaking of Darrell Boyd, Darrell Dontell Boyd, said Cyphus, my father, he said.

Aye, he cum round here campaignin, that's the one,

said the bartender. Pesterin' peoples 'bout votin' fur 'im, handin' ut the writin' pens and nail cutters.

Mr. Buck came back from the ladies' room, his clothes soaking wet, water dripping off his face onto the bar.

I fell in, he said.

But have you seen my father since? said Cyphus.

Seed the sum bitch onct since he disappeared like, cum in here dressed in a trash bag, I says tu him, Whut? Darrell, Howloween early dis year? You comin' round here dressed like a lyin' sack o' shit?

Haw! said the waiter.

Mr. Buck drained his special and set the empty glass down on the bar.

I loved the old man, the old man's like a father to me, he said, with chin quivering sentiment.

The bartender opened the cash register. Here's his 'ouse bill, he said. Yur here tuh pay, right? the bartender said, nodding to the rotten-tooth waiter. The bolt the waiter slid across the door was like Fort Apache, Cyphus thought.

Cyphus tipped the bill toward the light to read it. This is not his signature, he said.

Yup, he signed fur all the specials tha' night he cum

in, said the bartender, rolling a baseball bat along the edge of the bar top now.

The waiter took the saucer down off the top of the aquarium and went into a booth to chop up some lines with the fruit knife.

I never put the old man's car in the ditch, sobbed Mr. Buck. I put my own car in the ditch and I put my truck in the ditch but I never put the old man's car in the ditch, he said. Last time I put my car in the ditch somebody stole a cooler of fish out of the trunk, said Mr. Buck, his head up, remembering. When I come back with my truck to pull my car out of the ditch, the fish and the cooler was both gone.

The waiter snorted twice and then tinked the blade of the fruit knife on the edge of the saucer. The bartender looked over there and sniffed his upper lip.

Las' call, said the bartender and he wrote a bill for Mr. Buck.

What's this? he said.

Yur bill, says the bartender.

I wasn't finished drinking, said Mr. Buck. I didn't finish my special.

Ur finished, pay up, said the bartender.

Gottdamnit, said Mr. Buck.

Cyphus took all the money he had left in the world

and put it on the counter to pay his father's phony tab. He knew it was never going to be enough. Mr. Buck picked up the bills, ripped them into pieces, and threw them over the bartender's head like confetti.

There's your fucking tip, said Mr. Buck.

Everyone watched the bartender carefully shake his fingers in the sink, wipe his hands on a rag, and walk patiently around the end of the bar to take hold of Mr. Buck. He laid one hand on Mr. Buck's shoulder and then he pulled Mr. Buck's arm sharply behind his back.

Now I got you! said Mr. Buck. Mr. Buck twisted and spun around so that suddenly the bartender stood holding an empty, worn-out raincoat.

Every chicken white-meat muscle in Mr. Buck's shirtless trembling torso went into grabbing a stool and shoving it toward the bartender. Looking for something more substantial to fling, Mr. Buck tipped over to a large booth table that was bolted to the floor. His effort was so great, his buffalo-wing muscles gathering so much of what strength he still possessed, that in lifting the huge oak table over his head, he in fact merely jerked himself forward across the immovable tabletop, rapping soundly his forehead into unconsciousness, falling quickly and with no theatrics to the floor.

'E's nut dun thut before, considered the bartender, wadding up the raincoat and chucking it onto Mr. Buck.

Someone was kicking in the door.

Officer Westbrook and Samuel had crept up on the porch of the bar. From their vantage point, the little salt-crusted porthole in the front door, they had not seen the waiter with the fruit knife in the booth, but they *had* seen the softball bat rolling on the bartop and had seen Mr. Buck go down. Officer Westbrook had developed immensely powerful legs dune climbing, which were in fact his saving grace with his awful shrew wife when the kitchen-utensil throwing had ended and she had locked her ankles in that way behind his, and with these strong legs, when he had seen the bartender draw a peg-leg shotgun from under the bar and point it toward Cyphus fending off the fruit knife with the red plastic rake, Officer Westbrook kicked in the door.

Salt, neglect, and rust had corrupted the old shells in the peg-leg and it did not fire, so the bartender dropped it as Officer Westbrook covered the escape of Cyphus, his hand on his malignant-looking flashlight holster, pointing it alternately at the bartender and the waiter by cocking his hip first to the left and then to the right, backing carefully out of the Baja, careful not to trip on the splintered door cockeyed on the floor.

Follow us, said Officer Westbrook to Cyphus standing in the parking lot holding his rake in one hand and a wrist of Mr. Buck in the other. It had seemed the decent thing to do to drag the head-knocked and nattering limp figure out of the Baja and down the rough uneven steps. He wasn't even that heavy, really, and Cyphus was able to do it one-handed, thinking he would stuff Mr. Buck in the back of Officer Westbrook's jeep, but there it went in sand dust and taillights, and Cyphus was left with the little shirtless man. Cyphus was certain that if he left Mr. Buck in the parking lot by dawn a fish truck or a four-wheel-drive utility vehicle would flatten him into the muck, so Cyphus shoved the muttering Mr. Buck into the back of the limousine and in the darkness accidentally closed the door on his hand, wincing in compassion at the crunch.

the sand trails and taillights leading deep into the little park-preserve pony stables began to depress Cyphus even more than his crushing indifference to the high school football game on the limousine radio. Tie game, Marlins and Sharks. Officer Westbrook led them to the wild pony pens and corral where Boy Scouts earned merit badges breaking the little horses that were ridable and shooting and skinning the ones that were not.

Officer Westbrook wheeled the jeep into the turn-around near some plain plank stables. He may still be out, he said to Cyphus, let's go look.

Out where? said Cyphus. It was noisy when he killed the engine, crickets and bullfrogs and alligator bellows and the constant metal ripping of light industry echoed by the lowering marine layer blotting out the night sky. The marine layer was infected pink from the nearby industrial park's vapor lights, and the baseshaft of a thunderhead thickening in the northeast sky was tumid with brilliant stadium glare.

Cyphus cocked his ear toward dim crowd roar. Last week the Sharks' head cheerleader ran across the field and broke some girl's arm in the visitor's stands, Officer Westbrook said. Sometimes she comes out here and lays out naked, smoking dope. She says she's had two abortions. She wears spurs. She got a tattoo look like a man's organ.

Will we be required to disinter our father or will wild dogs fetch him piece by piece? said Cyphus.

Officer Westbrook disappeared into a place where things snorted and kicked. Cyphus turned to Samuel.

All right, if we get the wallet, we split it down the middle and part ways. I'll take the car back home and you can figure out your end with Smokey the Bear here, said Cyphus.

The car doesn't belong to you, said Samuel.

You can't drive, said Cyphus.

That's not the point, said Samuel.

Shhhhh! Officer Westbrook shushed them, coming out of the stables with his flashlight unholstered and turned to the dim, wide-reach setting. Your father will see you now, he said.

The very corpulent Darrell Dontell Boyd reclined against a pony blanket and hay in a feeding trough fixed to the open side of an empty shed, the sharp stamping of ponies in the corral raised dust in the lantern Officer Westbrook lit. Darrell Boyd's hair was wet and pushed back, his girth was swaddled in enormous Fruit of the Looms, his bare knees were scraped from recently negotiating a moderate surf and the uneven beach shelf. A large black plastic trash bag covered his shoulders like a shawl, and it was pinned at the throat with an office folder clip. He did not rise from the manger when Officer Westbrook brought forth Cyphus and

Samuel, he maintained his open-browed gaze toward the bolus of stadium glare burning in the northeast.

Father, Samuel said, approaching the manger. It was not necessary nor profitable to kneel, the manger being almost chest high. To kneel would put you beneath the scene in hoofprints.

Darrell Boyd reached out his hand toward his young son to confer some type of blessing. He then drew Officer Westbrook's ear close to his mouth and began whispering loudly in a language Cyphus's sensible ear cocked around, a confounding spectrum of speculative Yiddish, West Malaysian, and a latinated Cherokee.

Your father is happy to see you, too, Cyphus, said Officer Westbrook in a tone Cyphus felt was a little too condescending for his taste. Your father is happy you have come to witness the great revelations, sends his regards to the remaining family sitting in darkness, and wonders what's with the rake?

What's wrong with him, why doesn't he speak normally to me, said Cyphus.

He is speaking normally, Officer Westbrook said with a brilliant smile.

Now, look here, Pops, Cyphus said. This wouldn't be my first choice of a hide-out, but it somehow seems to suit you and, possibly, you'll be able to lose some weight in the process. The family has sent Samuel and myself out to look for some papers they believe you are carrying so it's best you just hand over your wallet.

Officer Westbrook laughed in Cyphus's face as Cyphus made a move toward Darrell Boyd.

What your father is bringing to the world is more precious than anything written on paper, Officer West-brook said. Your father has been chosen. Every night he swims out to the bottom of the sea where angels are prepar-ing for the second coming.

He can't swim, he almost drowned as a child, said Cyphus.

Officer Westbrook laughed again and adjusted the Hefty Cinch-Sak robe around Dontell Boyd's shoulders. Dontell Boyd gazed upon the fiery column of stadium light burning in the northeast.

At the bottom of the sea angels are collecting, sharp-ening their swords and shodding their feet to come march-ing out of the waves. They tell your father wonderful things, and give him the trinkets that man has cast upon the ocean floor, said Officer Westbrook.

They haven't by any chance found his wallet, have they? Cyphus asked.

No, said Officer Westbrook, but they have given him this, and Officer Westbrook pulled from his pocket a piece of gold.

Wow, a gold doubloon, said Samuel.

Let me see that, said Cyphus. Cyphus studied the crude piece of eight and immediately recognized it as the piece of slag metal spray-painted gold Darrell Dontell Boyd used to carry in his wallet to foil unsuspecting tourons sweeping the beaches with their metal detectors. It was a great game Darrell used to play on the beach for his friends looking on from the plate-glass windows of the Thunderbird Lounge. You would drop the slag in the path of the metal-sweeping short-pants black-socks touron and just before he'd reach it you step in and snatch it up announcing, A gold doubloon! Wow! Right here in the sand! Gosh, if I hadn't of just seen it I guess you'd have picked it up! Wow! A once-in-a-lifetime find! And the gallery in the Thunderbird would watch the touron rip his headphones off his livid-faced head and then fling the several-hundred-dollar metal detector into the surf, the shorts almost falling down with the effort, its pockets jingly with the summer's vacation treasure finds so far—a nickel and a quarter's worth of lost bathing-suit change and a rusted Holiday Inn room key.

This is nothing, Cyphus said, flipping the coin into Darrell's ample lap. I want the wallet this came from and I want it now.

A snarling and ratching near the gate set off some hindkicking among the horses, and the air went high with whinnies and then low with a distant Marlin score.

Somethin's in with the horses, said Officer Westbrook. Could be a panther!

The ponies galloped round and round the emerging panther presupposer, a little white shirtless man with a galaxy of gold flecks sparkling his puny chest, pasted there with bile and sour beer.

Somebody call off these dogs, gottdamnit, said Mr. Buck.

A small stampede of Chincoteague horse color suddenly broached the gate and charged Cyphus, trying to bite the SuperResilient tines with their terrible mouths. Several hundred pounds of horseflesh shouldered Cyphus backward into the manger at Dontell Boyd's feet.

Esso bactoro factum dicta funk, said Darrell.

That's a lie, said Cyphus, rolling white-eyed, regaining his wind, spitting straw. You . . . phonetic imposter!

Ogan block! commanded Darrell Boyd, standing. *Ogan block de yevuh ah here ruh!*

Officer Westbrook and Samuel fell to their knees in the dust, Samuel a little stiffly.

Do what he says, Samuel said to Cyphus as Cyphus rolled out of the trough.

I don't even *know* what he's saying, said Cyphus, Cyphus crawling around the perimeter of lantern light searching for his rake. Just as soon as he could lay his hands on its handle, he would use it to help send this, their father, back into the sea.

Osta la bean ba! announced Darrell Dontell Boyd.

It's another message from the First Jesus Under the Living Water! said Officer Westbrook. He's speaking in tongues! said Officer Westbrook. Isn't it wonderful?

Yes, yes, I hear it now! Cyphus said, standing, bouncing his tines in great anticipation. I can hear it, the summons of the Scuba Christ! he said, saying, to himself, Remember to be careful. The footing in the shorebreak will be crumbly this time of year, the undertow deceptively strong.

memorial day

The boy mistook death for one of the landlady's sons come to collect the rent. Death
stood leaning against a tree scraping fresh
manure off his shoe with a stick. The boy told
death he would have to see his mother about
the rent, and death said he was not there to
collect the rent.

My brother is real sick, you should come
back later, the boy said.

Death said he would wait.

They had sent the boy's brother home
from the war in a box. When the boy and his
mother opened the box, the brother was not
inside. Inside the box was a lifesize statue of a
woman holding a seashell to her ear. A mes-

senger's pouch hung around the statue's neck. Hide this for me, the note in the pouch read. Love, Brother.

Then came the brother a week later. He was thin and yellow and sorry-looking, too weak to fend off his mother when she struck him, too weak to be held. The mother and the child carried him into the house and put him to bed.

The next morning, a black healer woman walked down the white shell driveway and straight into the house to squeeze the older brother's guts and smell his breath. She looked over her shoulder at the high weeds and the statue box and the bitter, brown gulf beyond and she said, This place flood flood flood. Stink, too.

The mother bathed the brother with an alcohol sponge and the black healer woman twisted his spine to break his fever. The brother saw monkeys in the corners of the ceiling that wanted to get him, their mouths full of bloody chattering teeth. The black healer woman and the mother fought with the brother and told the child to Get out! when he came in to tell them that someone was waiting in the yard.

It was not unusual that the child could see death when the mother and the healing woman could not. Once, at a church picnic the child had seen Bad Bob Cohen walk through the softball game and past the barbeque tables with a .22 rifle slung barrel-down over his shoulder on a piece of twine. The child had watched Bad Bob walk right past where mothers and small children were splashing on the riverbank, had watched Bad Bob reach up and select two sturdy vines to climb up, and Bad Bob had turned and looked at the child, feeling him seeing him, and Bad Bob had nodded because they both knew that Bad Bob was invisible, and then later when the deputy and the road agents came to the picnic looking for Bob no one had seen him and no one would have believed the child if he had said he had, so he said nothing. Also, one Easter, the child had seen an angel.

Tell them they have to wait, the mother said. The rent's not due until tomorrow.

You have to wait, the child told death sitting in a tree. Death ate a fortune cookie from his pocket. His lips moved while he read the fortune to himself.

I'll come back tomorrow, death said finally, jumping down from the tree.

the black healer woman stood on the porch and said she would keep death from the doorstep as long as they had faith in Christ Jesus Our Savior and a little put-away money to cover her expenses coming down the long white broken-shell driveway to their house. Death, that day, was wearing white pants and a white dinner jacket, a small, furled yellow cocktail umbrella buttonholed in his lapel. There were three good scratches across death's cheek from the beautiful woman who had not wanted to dance the last dance with death aboard a ship somewhere the previous evening. I don't get much time off from this job, death confided in the child under the tree. Work work work. I am much misunderstood. I actually have a wonderful sense of humor and I get along well with others. I'm a people person, death told the child. Death climbed the front porch steps to make faces behind the black healing woman. Death folded his eyelids back, stuck out his tongue, then pinched his cheeks forgetting about the scratches. Ow! death said. The black healer woman did not hear death nor see death but to her credit, she shivered when death blew on the back of her neck.

The child followed the black healer woman and his mother into the back bedroom where his brother stank. The black healer woman burned some sage cones and rubbed charcoal on the brother's temples and on the soles of his feet to draw out the fever.

How come you don't work? the black woman said to the child.

He's just a child, the mother said. The mother was stripping the brother's bed around them to boil the sheets on the stove.

When I young, I work, said the black healing woman.

I can make baskets from reeds, the child said.

What do people need *reed* baskets for when they give wooden ones away for free at the tomato fields, said the woman.

When the brother sat up and shouted, Get the monkeys! the black healing woman said to him, Your little brother here going to get them monkeys, your little brother going to get them monkeys and put them under baskets, under *wooden* baskets, she said to the child. Won't no *reed* basket hold no monkey, she said, and the brother lay back down.

Here's the rent money, the mother said. I don't want anybody to come in the house while we get your brother's fever down. The child said, Yes ma'am. He took out the messenger pouch his brother had sent home in the box with the statue. It was *not* a purse. It had two long pockets and a waterproof pouch in case you had to swim a river.

The child put the rent money in the waterproof pouch because it had two good snaps on it.

When the landlady's son came to collect the rent, death told the child to ask for a receipt.

I want a receipt, the child told the landlady's son.

You want to be evicted? the landlady's son said. You want us to throw your sorry asses out on the highway?

Don't worry, death said, he's afraid he might catch what your brother has. He won't go in the house. Tell him you want a proper receipt, tell him to bring a proper receipt for the rent.

Before the child could say all that the landlady's son said, Give me the money I bet you got in that purse!

It's not a purse! the child said and yanked back on the strap.

All right, I'll be back tomorrow, said the landlady's son.

Death sat on the edge of the porch and lip-read a new fortune cookie. It looked like a word near the end hung him.

That's a good one, death finally said, and he crunched the cookie in his big white teeth.

---

the brother's tongue grew fuzzy and his ravings were barking up the bad neighbor's dogs down the road all night.

The black healer woman came out on the porch.

You get me a shoebox of scorpions, what I need, she told the child. Try get me white ones. They stronger than the piddly brown ones. Go on and get me them.

They had scorpions in the woodpile, scorpions in the sandbox, scorpions in the clothes-pin pouch, scorpions in the cinderblocks where they burned trash, scorpions under the bathroom sink, scorpions in the icebox water tray, and scorpions in the baby crib. They didn't have a baby any-more, so it was all right.

I wouldn't fool with scorpions, death said. Some peo-ple are highly allergic. It's a neurotoxin thing in the stinger, death said. Death followed the child around trying to find a shoebox. The child could not find a shoebox. He had an old wooden-style cigar box. The lid was broken.

I wouldn't use that cigar box, it's got no lid, death said. The child said he could see that.

The child took the rent money out of his waterproof pouch and put it in his pocket. He cut a good stick and found three brown scorpions and one white scorpion by lunchtime. He put the scorpions in the messenger pouch and snapped it shut carefully so not to crush them, and shook the bag down every time before he opened it so he would not get stung. He had never been stung before and had heard it was ten times worse than a wasp, maybe fifty times.

It looks to me like your brother's got a neural infection that may be at the stem of his brain, death said. Of course, that's just a layman's guess.

The child was beginning to tire of death hanging around so much and talking talking talking. Death never seemed to shut up. Down where the bitter brown gulf water foamed dirty, death talked about time zones and the speed of light. Under the big yard tree, he talked about pine cones that broke open their seeds only when they burned. Under the brother's window looking in on the mother and the black healer woman, death said the brown statue of the girl holding the seashell to her ear was pedestrian terracotta.

I bet it's valuable, the child said, and death said, Yeah, maybe as a boat anchor.

The mother took back the rent money to fetch a real doctor. The landlady's son came by with a friend who smelled like vomit and the friend who smelled like vomit threw a dirt clod that hit the child in the mouth. The landlady's son kicked open the front gate. The child had forgotten he had taken the rent money out of the messenger pouch so he held on to its strap until the landlady's son broke it and said, Here's your receipt, and he rabbit-punched the child twice in the ear. The landlady's son and the friend who smelled like vomit roared off in their car with the messenger pouch, taking with them, inside the pouch, the little yellow furled cocktail umbrella, twelve white scorpions, and thirty, maybe even fifty brown scorpions in the waterproof pocket. Death laughed in the treetops.

Death flocked down beside the child. He said maybe the scorpion cure would have worked and maybe it would have killed the brother outright. It would have depended on if the black healer woman could figure a good way to extract the neurotoxin and put the brother into moderate shock to break the fever. I guess it *could* work, maybe in a laboratory, death said, and the child, holding his ringing ear, said, You just want an easy way to take my brother from me, and death said the child had completely misunderstood him. That was all right, because he was much misunderstood, death began again, and maligned, and the child left death in the front yard making speeches, and to the child's one good ear, it all sounded like wind in the stovepipe.

the doctor hardly thought it worth breaking a car axle to drive down and look at the brother, so he took the rent money for his trouble walking and said to bathe the brother in alcohol and put these sulphate powders in honey tea. The doctor gave the brother a shot and on his way out said the child needed some fish oil but did not give him any.

You find them scorpions for me? the black healer woman whispered after the doctor had gone.

I had a bunch that got away from me, the child told her. She said to get her a new bunch unless he wanted his brother to die. To-night, she said. The black healing woman had no faith in the shot or the sulfate or the doctor. She said she had seen him swing little newborns by their heels against tree trunks back where the real white trash lived. Go get them scorpions and get them quick, she said.

Death sat on the levee pipe and watched the child

weave a reed basket. Death said baskets done well like that could fetch maybe two, three dollars from tourists. Of course, the child would have to learn to weave the popular check-cross design, and not just the standard lanyard double-tuck.

This is for scorpions, the child said. The child said he noticed death had not come around the house when the doctor came, and death laughed and said he liked doctors, that you could make a career following doctors. No, death said he had just had an appointment that had taken a little longer than he had planned for, and he offered the child a fortune cookie.

No thanks, said the child, weaving his basket.

Death read his fortune. Sometimes these things are incomprehensible, he said, and he let the little white paper float away.

That night the brother broke the mother's jaw. Punched her right in her damn monkey teeth, red and chattering at him.

no one knows their time. The brother recuperated and returned to the war, and afterward operated a small, profitable import business until his death at age fifty-eight from smoke inhalation. He had been trying to retrieve an old three-legged dog from a warehouse fire.

The man who smelled like vomit died of emphysema at age seventy-two living on the benevolence of the state. The state ridded itself of Bad Bob Cohen at age forty-one with a lethal injection.

It is believed among the black healing woman's family, and among those to whom she administered, that she was commended by God, that God spared her from death entirely, that He lifted her directly into heaven, for one day she simply disappeared.

The mother died seven years after the older brother recuperated. Her jaw did not heal well and her weight dropped to slightly below normal for her height, diet, and hereditary dispensation. The mother's passing away at age forty-eight was generally ascribed to grief, from finding her youngest remaining son at the edge of the hot brown gulf. According to the deputy and to the coroner who drove the station wagon to fetch the body, it appeared that the bottom of the reed basket the child had been carrying had flung itself open somehow, as if whoever had made the basket had folded the reeds backwards, upside down into the spiraling center instead of outward to the edges, and the action and weight of several hundred scorpions inside the basket had broken through the bottom. The child had been stung too many times to count. The neurotoxin, to which the child was highly allergic, had caused his wind-pipe to close, and when they found him at the edge of the gulf, he had already turned blue, his protruding tongue black and flyspecked. It was as if the child had run down to the gulf while being stung to drink the bitter water and could not drink, could not force down what he thought he felt he could not swallow, and only death had seen him try, death saying to him, Run to the water and drink, come on, run with me to the gulf and drink, and the child had taken death's outstretched hand because he was beginning to stumble, and death encouraged him, Run with me! and the child ran with death and finally he was no more, for death had taken him.

As for the landlady's son, he is one of many who have long since been forgotten.

For their generosity, grateful thanks to the estate of Tennessee Williams, to John and Renee Grisham, and to the Charles Hobson family.

For counsel, praise, threats, encouragement, loans, proclamations, cars, trucks, baby clothes, prayers, insurance, houses, and 3 A.M. dinners at Denny's: Tom Waits, Joe Kerr, Amy Hempel, Georges Borchardt, George Parker, Chase Crossingham, Margery Tabankin, Julie & Johnny, Susan & George, Kiersten & Bruce, Greg & Christine, Nan Talese, Gale Duke, Alice Sonnier, Elin Vanderlip, the Overtron Family, Etty, and Claire.

M.R.

about the author

mark richard is the author of the critically acclaimed novel *Fishboy* and the award-winning short story collection *The Ice at the Bottom of the World*, which won the PEN/ Ernest Hemingway Foundation Award. He is also the recipient of such distinguished honors as the Whiting Foundation Award, the Mary Francis Hobson Medal for Arts and Letters, and fellowships from the National Endowment for the Arts and the Tennessee Williams Foundation. His short stories have appeared in *Esquire*, *The New Yorker*, *Harper's*, *The Oxford American*, and *The Paris Review*, and have been widely anthologized in such publications as *Best American Short Stories*, *New Stories from the South*, and *The Pushcart Prize Annual*. He lives in Los Angeles, where he is working on a new novel.